His effect on her had been instant, shocking.

Even now, just one glance from those electric eyes brought back that rush of delirious wanting, those shivers of primal desire. But Sofia couldn't ignore the proof. Even that blinding haze of love, that frantic need to believe Luke, hadn't been enough to erase the facts. He'd used her to steal those gems.

But as she stood before him now, feeling his resentment, his rage, doubt slithered through her, and a sick, queasy sensation wormed into her gut. Why the outrage? If he'd been guilty, then why was he so angry at her, especially after all these years?

Could she have been wrong?

Dear Reader,

I've always wanted to set a book in Spain, a land steeped in contrasts—poetry and passion, flamenco music and bagpipes, Roman bridges and Celtic ruins. And when I discovered Luke Moreno prowling through a medieval palace, I knew I'd found the perfect hero for my book. Luke's as complex as the land he lives in, an honorable man with a shady past, a man who has spent his life fighting stereotypes and injustice—only to find himself framed for a theft.

Luke's emotions burn hot, and so do the sparks between him and his ex-lover Sofia Mikhelson, the woman he believes is setting him up. I had a great time following their breakneck trek through Spain as they hunted down the missing necklace and uncovered a tangled web of danger far more sinister than they'd dreamed.

I hope you enjoy Luke's journey, book one of THE CRUSADERS miniseries.

Happy reading!

Gail Barrett

HEART OF A THIEF

Gail Barrett

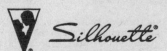

Silhouette®

Romantic

SUSPENSE

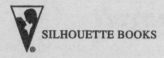

SILHOUETTE BOOKS

ISBN-13: 978-0-373-27584-7
ISBN-10:   0-373-27584-6

HEART OF A THIEF

Books by Gail Barrett

Silhouette Romantic Suspense

Facing the Fire #1414
*Heart of a Thief #1514

Silhouette Special Edition

Where He Belongs #1722

*The Crusaders

GAIL BARRETT

always dreamed of becoming a writer. After living everywhere from Spain to the Bahamas, raising two children, and teaching high school Spanish for years, she finally fulfilled that lifelong goal. Her writing has won numerous awards, including Romance Writers of America's prestigious Golden Heart. Gail currently lives in western Maryland with her two sons, a quirky Chinook dog and her own former Montana rancher/retired Coast Guard officer hero. Write to her at P.O. Box 65, Funkstown, Maryland 21734-0065, or visit her Web site, www.gailbarrett.com.

To my husband, John, for listening.

ACKNOWLEDGMENT:

I'd like to thank the following people for their help:
my critique partner, Judith Sandbrook, for her wonderful
insights; my sister, Mary Jo Archer, for reading and
critiquing my work; Marjorie Thelen for brainstorming
and commiserating with me, especially during the low
times; S.A. Stone for his safecracking tips; and Rosa and
Yoshi Takebe for answering my endless questions and
driving me around Galicia. *Miles de gracias.* Thank you!

When the full moon bleeds and the lonely dog cries
And the stars trail dust in the night
A leader will rise from the scattered hordes
And the People will regain their might.
> —*Indian poem, circa 1000 A.D.*

Chapter 1

The blonde sauntered into view on the security monitor, looking like every erotic dream he'd ever had—sultry, seductive, sin-on-heels sensuous. Luke Moreno's pulse hitched, and a wild laugh rose in his throat. Oh, yeah. This woman was his fantasy, all right. His Delilah. His Mata Hari. His Eve in the Garden of Eden.

Too bad she was just as corrupt.

He watched, riveted, as she approached the glass display case cordoned off with velvet ropes. She played the elegant guest role to perfection, bending close to admire the primeval amber, the meticulously hammered gold. As if she'd never

seen the ancient necklace before. As if she hadn't come here
to steal it. As if she weren't setting him up to take the blame—
again.

Damn her conniving soul.

"Who let her in here?" he demanded, still not pulling his
eyes from the screen.

"Who?" Luke's partner in his security business, Antonio
Flores, leaned across the crowded console toward the
monitor.

"*La americana.* Sofia Mikhelson."

His partner raised one stocky arm, reached for the laptop
nearby and tapped the keyboard to scroll down the names. "Mikhelson. Sofia. She's on the list. Part of the antiquities crowd."

"She wasn't on the list last night."

"We added a new batch this morning." Antonio leaned
back in his chair and lifted his hands, palms out. "You know
how it's been. We've had experts calling from all over the
world. It's been a nightmare trying to vet them all."

Luke grunted. He couldn't argue that. It wasn't often a
thousand-year-old necklace surfaced in a Spanish bank
vault—especially this necklace. The Gypsy's Revenge, coveted for centuries, shrouded in legends, haunted by an ancient
curse—a curse that condemned any non-Gypsy who touched
it to die. An artifact so elusive, so priceless, so powerful that
few experts even believed it existed until now.

But the necklace was real, all right, and sitting in that
case—a dazzling gold collar inscribed with ancient symbols,
inlaid with multi-hued amber, adorned with miniature bells.
And its discovery had ignited a firestorm of controversy—
former Nazi war loot, Swiss banking connections—an inter-
national scandal ready to explode. Now every antiquities
expert on the planet had converged on the palace outside of
Madrid demanding a close-up look.

But this woman hadn't come here to admire the necklace. His gaze hardened on the lush curves sheathed in the black satin gown, the gleam of her naked back, that slow, smoldering smile that still incinerated his nerves like lightning scorching parched earth.

No, she hadn't come here to view the necklace. Sofia Mikhelson was as deceptive as the forgeries she made. Exquisite, enthralling, alluring—but fake.

Anger whipped through his gut.

"The ceremony's about to start," he told Antonio, the raw heat making his voice clipped. "I'm going to check out the crowd. Keep your eye on that necklace."

A tense buzz rising in his ears at the thought of Sofia, he stalked from the brightly lit office and headed down the carpeted hallway past dark, massive portraits of centuries' worth of Spanish nobility as cameras winked from silk-lined walls.

It had taken him five years to salvage his reputation. Five years battling suspicions and accusations, fighting the arrogance of power, the tyranny of wealth.

And now he had everything riding on this ceremony—his career as a security expert, his honor, his pride. This was his one chance to finally redeem himself, to prove himself to the world.

The muscles along his jaw bunched while resentment seared in his chest. He'd played the fool once with that woman. It had ended with his illusions shattered and his reputation destroyed. No way would he do it again.

No matter what she had planned.

He strode into the throne room, paused, then skipped his gaze across the crowd shimmering beneath the chandeliers, their tumult of languages muted by the thick Belgian rugs. He arrowed in on Sofia, poised just meters from the ancient necklace, and adrenaline rushed through his gut.

The game's on, querida. And he was going to win.

Keeping his eyes locked on that golden hair, he wove through the maze of celebrities and politicians, billionaires and pedigreed nobles—all gathered to witness the historic moment when the Spanish government returned the long-lost necklace to the Roma people.

"Señoras y señores," the Duke of Zamora began at the podium. The crowd hushed, and Luke spared a glance at the royal Roma family now standing behind the necklace, palace guards posted discreetly to the side. *"Es con gran honor y placer que les presento…"*

Luke ignored the duke's welcome and swung his gaze back to Sofia. With a few long strides, he closed the distance between them, then positioned himself slightly behind her, close enough to watch her inhale, to catch any movements she made.

Too close. Before he could stop it, his gaze dipped and traced the curve of her back, the feminine swell of her hips. And those unwanted memories came blasting back—the heat of her lips, the salt of her skin, that small, provocative hitch in her breath when her eyes turned to molten green.

The quick pull in his groin caught him off guard. He grimaced, tugged at his tuxedo collar, and forced his gaze back up. So his body still responded to her. That just proved that morals had nothing to do with sex.

Because no way did this woman have a conscience.

He made a rough, low sound of disgust, and she turned her head. Her eyes met his and widened on a flash of surprise. As if she hadn't expected him here. Or she didn't think he'd have the nerve to confront her?

"Luke?" she whispered, sounding stunned.

He tipped his head. "Sofia." His voice came out deep, raw, graveled by five years of rage.

She blinked, then nibbled her lip, and he watched emotions parade through her gray-green eyes—uncertainty, guilt, doubt.

Good. About time she started to feel nervous.

"I…I didn't think you… I mean, I thought you…" She stopped, inhaled. "I mean, this is nice. I—"

"Nice." He tried out the word, then bit back a bitter laugh. "Yeah, I'll just bet it is."

Her lips closed. A flush crept up her cheeks, and her eyes flickered with a new emotion. Hurt? What did she have to feel wounded about? *She'd* come here to destroy *him*. Again.

It was a nice touch, though, making her look vulnerable. Innocent. Five years ago he would have fallen for it, too.

But then her chin rose, her soft lips firmed into a brittle smile, and once again she was the princess of the antiquities world, the premier expert on ancient amber. Lofty, composed, reserved—except for that small nervous gesture as she tucked a strand of hair behind her ear.

The corner of his mouth kicked up, and his gaze drilled into hers. *Ah,* querida. *Never try to fool your former lover.* He knew her too damned well.

She whirled back around, her spine suddenly rigid, and whispered to the short man beside her. Luke shifted his gaze to her escort, and everything inside him went still. Don Fernando Heredia. Sofia's patron. The man she'd trusted more than him.

Of course he'd be here. He would have planned this heist. Fitting task for a high-bred noble, a model of culture and wealth.

The small man turned to Luke, and their gazes locked. For an eternity neither moved, neither looked away, two old enemies mired in combat. But then don Fernando lifted his brows and tilted his head, the gesture aloof, politely condescending—exactly how a rich, powerful man would greet the Gypsy scum he'd accused of stealing his gems.

Luke's pulse drummed in slow, dull beats, and the edges of his vision dimmed. He curled his hands, aching to avenge the injustice, the prejudice, the futility of spending a lifetime battling his way out of poverty only to see his efforts destroyed.

But this wasn't the time. Not yet. Not here. He sucked in his breath, then squeezed it back out. He forced his shoulders down, flexed his fingers and pressed them to his thighs, beating back the humiliation, the fury, the shame. He unclenched his jaw and rocked back on his heels, willing his mind to clear and his pulse to ease. He couldn't afford to let his anger distract him.

Not with this much at stake.

Just then a movement in his peripheral vision caught his attention, and he jerked his gaze to the side. His pulse instantly sprinted again and he searched the crowd, but no one moved, nothing seemed out of place. The duke droned on at the podium. The royal Roma couple—official representatives of the Gypsy people—waited to receive the necklace. Their daughter, the princess, stood behind them. The guests listened and watched, their expectation mounting as the moment to remove the necklace from the case neared.

To see if the deadly curse would come true—that any non-Gypsy who touched it would die.

Luke waited a beat, then exhaled. Sofia and her patron had made him too damned jumpy. But something was about to happen; he could feel it. The hairs on the nape of his neck rose. Anticipation pulsed in the air. He ran his gaze over the guests, wary, alert.

Then suddenly, a man vaulted over the velvet ropes, his flushed face and wild eyes at odds with his formal tuxedo. "*¡Que mueran los gitanos!*" he shouted and whipped out a gun.

Death to the Gypsies? Luke's heart stalled as the man pointed the weapon at the royal couple. The stunned silence shattered with two sharp pops.

The couple fell. A woman screamed. Palace guards surged forward, their weapons drawn. More guns barked and the murderer dropped.

Chaos broke loose. Around Luke people panicked, screamed, scattered and shoved their way toward safety, all pretense of civility gone. Guards leaped to surround the stunned princess. Others raced to block the exits and protect the necklace, just as they'd been trained.

His own heart hammering, his pulse rocketing through his veins with a violent buzz, Luke spun back toward Sofia. Her patron still stood there, looking suitably shocked.

But Sofia was gone.

He swept his gaze through the frantic crowd. Where was she? Why hadn't she tried to steal the necklace? Unless the one on display was a fake…

His stomach dipped. Oh, hell. Where had she gone?

Cursing his stupidity, he raced toward the door with the frenzied guests, shouldering them out of his way. Then he pushed ruthlessly through the bottleneck crowding the exit, paused and scanned the hall. He glanced right, then left, just as a blond woman rounded the corner and disappeared.

His pulse leaped, and he gave chase. She had several yards on him, but he was faster, especially with her tight gown and spiked heels impeding her pace. He bolted down the hall and sprinted around the corner just seconds after she did, catching up in a few long strides. Furious now, he grabbed her arm, jerked her around and shoved her against the wall.

"Where is it?" he demanded. He gripped her arms and leaned against her, blocking her in with his weight. Behind him several guards rushed past, their guns drawn and radios squawking, shouting instructions and commands.

"What? Where's what?" She struggled uselessly against him, her chest heaving, her eyes pools of panic and fear. "Luke, let go! That man…the gun—"

"The necklace. Where is it?" He tightened his hands and gave her a shake, and her eyes whipped back to his. "And I don't mean the fake."

"But it's…" A flush stained her cheeks. Her breath rasped in uneven pants. Confusion edged out the fear in her eyes. "You know where it is. In the safe in the library, right where Antonio put it. Where else would it be?"

Antonio? He blinked, shook his head. What did his partner have to do with this? They'd never discussed the need for a decoy to fool potential thieves. This woman was just trying to distract him. And he didn't have time for these games. "Prove it."

Ignoring her protests, intent on finding that necklace before his career was destroyed, he dragged her down the hall, not caring that she had to jog to keep up with him. He towed her through a store room and detoured down another hallway, while questions spun through his brain. Who would want to kill the Roma royals? A terrorist? Or was their shooting just a distraction for the theft?

He stopped at an unmarked door, released her long enough to unlock it with his master key, then grabbed her bicep again. "Let's go."

The temperature dropped as they entered the oldest part of the palace, an area off limits to guests—a section the security cameras didn't reach. The musty air, water-stained ceilings and threadbare carpets reflected years of disuse and neglect.

But Luke knew every stone, every crack in this medieval

fortress. He'd spent months memorizing the layout, checking for weak points, scouring the dungeon and ancient bolt-hole, making sure no terrorists could worm in—never suspecting that the real danger would come from inside.

He stopped in front of the huge door leading to the library, its ornate carvings and inlaid panels layered with dust. Cautious now, aware that this could be a setup, he turned the knob, then kicked the massive door open. When nothing moved, he gave Sofia a short, sharp tug and pulled her inside.

He let go of her arm, closed the door, and scanned the room. The vaulted chamber looked empty, except for a few stray pieces of furniture and the cases of books.

"Which safe?" he asked, his skepticism rising. There were two antiquated wall safes in the room, neither secure enough for current use.

"Behind the painting. The one by the fireplace," she said.

He strode over to a small lamp perched on a table and flicked it on, then turned toward the fireplace. The dim light threw shadows on the frescoed ceiling and illuminated the paintings on the walls.

"You mean the Pacheco?"

"So you know art."

He scowled. Did she have to sound so surprised? He'd left the slums of El Salobral a lifetime ago. "A thief's got to be able to identify the loot, right, Sofia?"

Her eyes flashed. "You would know."

He hissed out his breath in disbelief. "You're not still trying to pin that on me?"

"But you did steal it. Don Fernando showed me—"

"Yeah, right." Disgusted, fighting back the futile rage that heated his blood, he crossed the room to the painting. There was no point trying to defend himself. She'd chosen to believe Don Fernando over him long ago.

But her disloyalty still rankled.

Anxious to end this farce, he turned his attention to the safe. He found the hinge in the gilded frame easily enough and swung the painting out from the wall. But when he examined the lock—an old-fashioned disk tumbler—suspicion again crawled through his gut. Why leave a priceless artifact in an unguarded safe—one with a lock a beginner could crack? Nothing about this made sense.

Unless this was a trap. His unease mounting, he swiveled his gaze back to Sofia. She was rubbing her arms, scanning the room. From nerves or guilt?

"What's the combination?" he asked her.

"I don't know. I don't!" she protested when he shot her a dangerous look. "I just made the decoy. Ask Antonio. I brought it here early this evening, he swapped it for the original, and that was it."

"The hell he did."

"But…he did." Her mouth sagged. "You don't think that I…"

Damn right he did. Fed up now, he stalked back to her, moving too close, invading her space. Then he gripped her chin and tugged it up, forcing her eyes to his. "I wouldn't suggest lying to me, *querida*."

"I'm not lying," she gritted out. Her cheeks were flushed. Her nostrils flared. Outrage sparked in her eyes.

His gaze held hers. She didn't waver, didn't blink.

Five years ago he would have believed her. Then again, five years ago he would have crawled through fire for this woman.

He was a lot smarter now.

He admired her acting ability, though. She had that fervent indignation, that innocent sincerity part down pat.

Wondering how far she'd take this game, he stroked his thumb down her throat, tracing the path his mouth once took.

Her eyes turned narrow and dark; her pulse quivered beneath his hand. He lowered his gaze to her lips—moist, lush, tempting—and heard that ragged hitch in her breath.

His own heart kicked in response.

He hissed out his breath and stepped back. This woman was trouble. Dangerous. A distraction he couldn't afford.

Scowling, he strode back to the safe. He dragged in a breath and exhaled, forcing his pulse to calm, his heart to slow, driving the carnal need from his blood.

"What are you going to do?" she asked.

"Crack the safe." He glanced back. "Unless you want to share that combination after all?"

Her forehead wrinkled. "But I told you, Antonio—"

"Right." Fed up with her deception, he turned back to the safe. He flexed his hands, loosened his shoulders, waited until his hands were steady, his breathing calm. Then he reached for the dial.

His attention focused completely on the lock, he turned the dial, closing his eyes to feel the movement of the drive cam. He concentrated, slowly moved the dial, working to align the lever to the groove in the wheel. Sensing, feeling, listening.

Acting like the thief he used to be.

The thief too many believed he still was.

The first wheel clicked into place.

"*Por aquí.* In here," a man said outside the library door.

Luke's heart stopped. He opened his eyes and sliced his gaze to Sofia. Her eyes widened, and she bit her lip.

Suspicion rolled through him. Were those her partners? Had she been heading here all along? "Expecting someone?"

"What? Of course not." Fear edged out the indignation in her eyes. "But…that gunman. You don't think there are more…?"

He straightened. They couldn't wait here to find out. And he couldn't leave Sofia alone in case she tipped them off.

He swung the painting back into place. "Come on," he whispered and grabbed her arm.

"Where?" she whispered back.

He glanced at the door to the adjoining room. Too far; they'd never make it. And the sofa wouldn't provide any cover with those tall, clawed feet.

He looked at the high arched windows blackened by the night, their long, velvet drapes tied back with braided cords. It might be an obvious place to hide, but they didn't have much choice.

"Over here." He pulled her to the nearest window, then turned and unhitched the tie-back cords. The thick, heavy drapes closed around them, plunging them into darkness, cocooning them in dust and heat.

Unwilling to trust her, he tightened his arm around her waist and pulled her tightly against him. He clamped his other hand over her mouth.

"Don't move," he warned and felt her nod.

The library door squeaked open and they both stilled. "It's by the fireplace," the voice said again, and Luke's heart went numb. Antonio, his partner. The man he'd thought he could trust.

Betrayed again.

"You'd better hurry," another man said and this time, Sofia jerked. So it was someone she recognized. No surprises there. He'd figured that she was involved.

"Claro." Antonio again.

Footsteps tapped across the marble floor. The heat built behind the musty drapes, and sweat trickled down Luke's jaw. Sofia stirred slightly, adjusting her position, and he inhaled the familiar spice of her hair, felt her hot breath fanning his palm, her satin-clad bottom caressing his groin.

Dumb move, Moreno. He winced, shifted to ease the sudden arousal he knew she could feel, and peered through the slit in the drapes. His partner, Antonio, was opening the safe with latex gloves while a hulking, balding man waited beside him. Luke frowned, trying to place the man, and then it clicked. Paco, don Fernando's bodyguard. He'd seen him at don Fernando's estate.

But what was the bodyguard doing here with Antonio? And suddenly, realization slammed through him, a sick, dizzy feeling reeling through his head. No wonder he'd gotten this job. It had nothing to do with his reputation, nothing to do with his skill or his hard work paying off. What a fool he had been. He'd been hired because Antonio had connections to don Fernando, a politically powerful man.

And now he was being set up—by Antonio, this bodyguard, don Fernando, probably even Sofia. They were all in on this plan.

And he was the perfect target—a Gypsy with a criminal background. No one would doubt his guilt.

"*Ya*," Antonio said as he opened the safe. He pulled out a black velvet pouch containing ancient necklace, opened it and grinned. Even from a distance, Luke could see the triumph on his face.

But then the bodyguard stepped behind Antonio, drew his gun and pressed it against his head.

Luke's heart stopped. Sofia turned rigid in his arms.

Across the room, Antonio's smile froze, faded. His eyes bulged, his mouth slackened, like a fish splayed at the local *mercado*.

No one moved. The air settled, condensed, suddenly too thick, too hot to breathe. Silence swelled like a primal shriek.

The sharp pop exploded in the stillness. Sofia gasped, and Luke tightened his hand on her mouth—too late. The killer swiveled toward the curtains and raised his gun.

Luke stared down the barrel of the SIG, and the hairs on the nape of his neck rose. Only his heart went berserk, thundering, lunging, careening in his chest, slamming the blood through his skull.

Damn. He'd known this woman was trouble.

And now, because of her, he was going to die.

Chapter 2

Sofia's nerves quaked. Her blood pounded through her skull with a terrified rush. She stared into the killer's eyes—black, cold, *aware*—and her stomach plummeted, freefalling into hysteria.

He'd heard her gasp. He knew they were here, hiding behind the curtains.

And now he was going to kill them.

Run! The command sliced through her frenzied brain, frantic, a shriek of delirious fear. But her limbs were rigid, petrified into place.

Paco stepped toward them, and her panic swelled. Dread churned from her belly to her throat, swamping it with bile. She gasped for air, tugging in fast, ragged pants but Luke's hand pressed against her mouth, and the drapes squeezed down, strangling the breath from her lungs. Terror reeked from her pores.

"*¿Han buscado aquí?*" a voice called from the hall, and the killer paused. His eyes narrowed, as if he were weighing, calculating, and then he glanced at the library door.

Sofia's pulse stuttered, and a crazed hope spun through her head. Let him leave. Oh, God, please let him leave.

But he turned back.

They were going to die. There was no way out. Only Luke's iron arm pinning her waist and the muscled wall of his chest kept her from collapse.

But then Paco bent and scooped the black velvet pouch from the floor. He stepped around Antonio and strode from view.

Through the thundering of her pulse she heard his footsteps recede, the snick of the door as it closed.

Nothing moved.

She didn't breathe.

Then Luke loosened his arm and dropped his hand. And she grabbed the drape and sucked in air, gulping, heaving, while a disjointed trembling invaded her limbs. *Oh, God. They'd nearly died.*

"Let's go." Luke's low voice rasped near her ear. He pushed her toward the curtains, and she stumbled out, hardly able to move.

Her skin felt chilled. Her heart still hammered in her chest. And her head seemed light, off-kilter, as if not quite connected to her neck.

Luke strode over to Antonio and dropped to one knee. His wide shoulders strained beneath his tuxedo. His black hair gleamed in the dim light.

He rolled the man over, loosened his tie, and held his fingers to his throat. He waited a beat, then ripped open Antonio's shirt and bent his head.

Sofia inched closer as he looked up. His grim, cognac-colored eyes met hers. "He's dead."

She opened her mouth to answer, but the stench of blood made her stomach roil. She managed a nod, wrapped her arms around her waist, avoided looking at Antonio's head. Instead, she glanced lower, to the black crescent-shaped tattoo exposed on his chest.

A weird thing to notice at a time like this. And so insignificant when the man was dead. *Dead.*

As if that ancient curse had come true.

She pressed her trembling hand to her lips, shuddered hard, willed that crazy thought away. The entire night had been a shock. The horrific murders, the theft. She swayed again, hugging herself harder to quell the hysteria rising inside. That beautiful, magical necklace was gone.

And seeing Luke after all this time. Luke—the man she'd once loved beyond reason. The man who'd enthralled her with his safe-cracking talent, mesmerized her with his brilliant mind.

The man who now scowled at her with rage and bitterness in his whiskey-hued eyes.

She eyed the implacable lines of his face, his unyielding jaw, that feral maleness that even now—even after all that pain—made everything primitive inside her go wild.

He rose to his feet in a powerful movement and stalked across the library to the door. Her stomach balled at the anger pounding his steps. Surely he didn't blame her for Antonio's death?

He pressed his ear to the door, waited, then edged it open and peeked out. "It's clear. Come on." His words were curt, clipped.

She forced aside the stab of hurt. His opinion of her didn't matter right now, and neither did their past. They needed to get out of here, get to safety. Warn don Fernando about Paco. Report the murder and theft. Because if that killer came back...

She shivered, then hurried across the library to the door.

Even with her high heels on, she had to look up to meet Luke's eyes. "Which way should we go?"

He eased the door shut again. His mouth was grim, the hard, shadowed planes of his face taut. "They'll have the exits blocked. We'll have to leave through the medieval bolt-hole."

She blinked. "What? We can't leave the palace. We have to find the police."

He shot her a look of disbelief. "And let them arrest us?"

"Arrest us?" Shock rippled through her. "But why would they do that? We haven't done anything wrong."

"You think they'll believe that?"

"Yes, of course. Why wouldn't they?"

His dark brows rose. "Because *you* made the replica. Because *I'm* in charge of security. Because my prints are now on that safe—and that's my partner lying there dead. Of course they're going to suspect us."

"But we didn't do anything wrong. Antonio arranged it all. And I made the decoy to fool potential thieves, not to steal the necklace."

"Right." He jerked his head toward the safe. "You think he'll testify on your behalf?"

She glanced back at Antonio's body, his head lying in a puddle of blood, and her gut made a sickening roll. He was right. "But other people know. Don Fernando—"

"Don Fernando?" He made a sound of disgust. "You can't be that naive. Who do you think set this up?"

"That's ridiculous. Don Fernando would never—"

"Never what?" He leaned toward her, his jaw rigid, anger sparking his eyes. "Never lie? Never fake a theft? Never frame some *Gypsy scum* for a crime he didn't commit?"

She lifted her palms, eased out her breath. "Look, I know you don't like him—"

"Like him?" His laugh was bitter, raw. He moved closer and fury radiated from him in waves. "That man ruined everything I'd ever worked for. My reputation, my career. Hell, if he hadn't *graciously* dropped the charges, I'd be in prison right now for something I didn't do."

And she'd sided with don Fernando. She heard the anger whipping his voice, the blame. He thought she should have supported him.

Her stomach twisted. She'd wanted to believe him. Dear God, how she'd wanted to believe him. She'd loved him desperately, insanely. He'd been her world, the most amazing man she knew.

His effect on her had been instant, shocking. Even now, just one glance from those electric eyes brought back that rush of delirious wanting, those shivers of primal desire.

But she couldn't ignore the proof. Even that blinding haze of love, that frantic need to believe him hadn't been enough to erase the facts. He'd used her to steal those gems.

But as she stood before him now, feeling his resentment, his rage, doubt slithered through her, and a sick, queasy sensation wormed into her gut. Then why the outrage? If he'd been guilty, then why was he so angry at her, especially after all these years?

Could she have been wrong? Dread spiraled through her, and she forced the thought from her mind. She couldn't bear to think of that now.

"Look," he said. His deep voice vibrated with disgust. "I'm leaving. You can hang around here if you want. Wait for the bodyguard to come back and kill you. Or wait for the police, so you can explain about the corpse."

Her stomach dipped. "They won't blame us for that?"

"I don't know what they'll do." His eyes stayed hard, accusing. "I don't even know who's involved here."

Meaning he still didn't fully trust her.

Sofia tamped back a sharp jab of hurt. She understood his suspicions. She felt just as confused. But she had nothing to do with that theft. She'd never endanger that necklace.

And neither would don Fernando. That man was too kind, too generous to hurt anyone, and he cared far too deeply about antiquities to ever arrange a theft.

But Luke was right about one thing. Other than Paco, they didn't know who was involved in this, which meant that they had to be careful.

She tugged in her breath, then exhaled. "Okay, you're right. We'd better hide." At least until the killer was caught.

"Keep quiet," he cautioned and opened the door. "And stay close."

As if he needed to warn her. That killer was out there. Her gaze flicked around the deserted hallway, and uneasiness crept through her chest. He could be lurking in a side room, just waiting for them to pass....

Luke took off, and she scurried behind him, cursing the tight gown and flimsy shoes that hindered her movements, the way her high heels clicked on the marble floor, the stark *tat-tat-tat* echoing down the corridor like a nervous drum.

They passed through unused rooms, detoured down endless halls, and with every step, her anxiety built. Her breathing turned shallow and fast. That awful pounding returned to her head. She hugged Luke's steps, seeking the safety of those wide shoulders, wanting to disappear into his skin.

Then, without warning, he stopped. He held out his muscled arm, and she bumped against him, barely staying upright.

"What?" she whispered. Her pulse notched up. Her heart shifted into her throat.

"Shh," he hissed, and she heard a voice in the hallway ahead.

A familiar voice. Her breath rushed out. She sagged and pressed her hand to her chest. "It's don Fernando." Thank goodness she'd found him. Now she could tell him what Paco had done.

But Luke grabbed her arm. "This way. Hurry up."

"Wait." She pulled her arm free, and he stopped. "I need to talk to him."

His eyes filled with disbelief. "You've got to be joking."

"No, listen." She stretched out her hand, but a flush climbed up his dark cheeks. And then he moved farther away.

"Luke, please," she said, but he took another step back. Her stomach plunged. He didn't understand. He probably thought she was going to betray him. And she didn't have time to explain.

She glanced up the hall, and a sick flutter formed in her throat. She needed to leave with Luke. She understood that.

But she couldn't abandon don Fernando. She owed her patron everything, more than Luke could know—her education, her career. He'd given her the opportunity to follow her dream, acceptance into the antiquities world, the only home she'd ever known.

"I just need a second," she said. "I just have to tell him…"

But Luke only turned and stalked off.

She watched him disappear into a side room, torn by the overwhelming urge to race after him, to shelter herself in his strength. To beg him to listen, to trust her, to let her explain.

But she couldn't turn her back on the man who'd helped her, the man who'd been like a father to her. She forced her gaze back to the hall where she'd heard her patron. She only needed to warn him, just whisper a word and then go.

She swallowed, slipped off her shoes to lessen the noise, then inched forward and pecked around the corner. A policeman, a *guardia civil* in a khaki green uniform stood several yards away, talking to another man. Don Fernando? She couldn't tell from this angle; the *guardia* blocked her view. But hadn't she just heard her patron's voice?

She hesitated, even more uncertain now. After what Luke said, she didn't dare involve the police. But she still had to warn don Fernando.

But then the *guardia* wheeled around and pulled out his gun. *"Pare. No se mueva,"* he commanded.

Don't move? Her heart faltered, and she froze. What was he doing? Why did he have his weapon trained on her?

Feeling surreal, as if her world had just spun loose, she gaped at the *guardia civil.* "I didn't do anything wrong," she protested. *"No hice nada."*

But then Paco sauntered forward, and her throat closed. Her heart nearly popped from her chest.

The killer. Oh, God. He was here.

And where was don Fernando?

Paco stopped beside the policeman, and his black eyes settled on hers. Her palms turned moist. Fear coursed through her, flooding her cells, blanking her mind.

For an eternity, his eyes stayed on hers—brittle, cold, deadly. Then recognition flared.

He knew.

Her stomach pitched. The walls pushed down. A dull ringing clanged in her skull.

He drew his gun. The gun he'd used to kill Antonio. Her mind flashed to Antonio's terrified eyes, the blood oozing from his flesh.

The bodyguard raised his gun, squinted one eye. And she knew he was going to shoot.

Her nerves zapped; adrenaline blazed through her blood. She whirled, raced around the corner toward the room where Luke had gone. *"Alto!"* the *guardia* shouted, and her panic surged.

A gun went off. Fierce fire scorched through her calf. She gasped, staggered, nearly fell. She'd been shot!

Her leg buckled and burned. She cried out at the vicious pain. But footsteps hammered behind her, and she forced herself to rush on.

Mercifully, the door Luke had gone through hung open, and she dashed inside. She glanced around frantically, but he wasn't there. A wild sob formed in her throat. "Luke! Luke!" Where on earth had he gone?

Panicking, she raced through the room to the opposite door, then tore down another long hall. Her lungs seared. Her heart went wild. The agony in her leg blurred her sight. And she knew she couldn't last. They were going to catch her. She was going to die.

Then a man stepped out from a doorway, and she shrieked. *Luke.* He grabbed her arm, jerked her into the room, then slammed and locked the door.

His face looked dangerous, the angles more rigid than she'd ever seen. He didn't pause. He yanked her along, crossing to the far wall, muttering a stream of obscenities in Spanish.

At the wall, he released her arm. She heaved in air. Her body shook. Blazing heat flamed through her calf.

He pulled back an ancient tapestry and shoved it toward her. "Hold this out of the way." It wasn't a request.

Her heart still ramming against her rib cage, she grabbed the tapestry and pulled it back. He ran his hands over the wooden panels on the wall, searching, glowering.

She heard a sound in the hall and glanced back. The doorknob rattled. Someone banged on the wood. Fear plucked at her nerves, constricted her throat. They had to get out of here—fast.

Luke pulled one of the panels, and her gaze swung back. A small door opened, exposing a dark passage carved through the stone. The ancient bolt-hole. Cold, musty air wafted out.

"Get in," he said.

Knowing she had no choice, she ducked and stepped inside. The freezing stones were a shock on her bare feet, and she realized she still clutched her shoes. But the shoes would have to wait; there was no room to maneuver inside the passage, barely enough to creep through. The dank, clammy space had obviously been chiseled from the stone for a desperate escape if disaster loomed.

She shuddered. This night had been a disaster, all right. She'd been chased. Nearly arrested. Shot.

Luke crouched and followed her into the passage. His broad shoulders brushed against the walls. He dug a penlight out of his pocket and held it out. "Hold this."

She took it, and he closed the door.

They were instantly plunged into darkness. She twisted the pen, and the narrow light came on, gleaming off the uneven stones.

Still shivering, she looked at Luke. He loomed close in the too-small space. The heat from his powerful body radiated to hers. In the faint light, the shadows blackened the hollows of his cheeks, turning the grim planes stark.

Her gaze met his, and her breath shriveled up. Her heart made a feeble throb.

She'd never seen him so enraged.

Could this night get any worse?

Chapter 3

Luke wanted to plow his fist through the wall.

Twice now Sofia had blitzed into his life, and each time she'd wreaked total disaster. She'd demolished everything he'd ever worked for—his reputation, his honor, his pride.

He glowered at her, his face hot, the muscles of his neck stiff. Hell. This time she'd done far worse than ruin his reputation. She'd put the police on his tail—and not just for the theft of a legendary antiquity but for *murder*. And now she'd led them to where he hid.

"Just what were you thinking back there?" he demanded.

Her eyes looked hurt in the faint light, and she tugged on a loose strand of hair. "I thought it was don Fernando. I wanted to warn him about Paco."

"I told you not to trust him."

"But he could be in danger. And I owe him so much. What do you expect me to do? Just…abandon him?"

The words crashed through him, kicking the breath from his lungs. "Right." Of course she couldn't abandon her patron.

But five years ago, she'd had no trouble abandoning *him*.

He jerked his gaze away, inhaled. And he struggled to hold on to his anger, to cling to the safety of rage. But that dead, hollowed-out feeling still surged through him, that emptiness that mauled him inside. As if she'd gutted him and bled him dry.

Shut it down. Shut it down. He didn't care. He refused to care.

He sucked in more air and hitched it back out. And gradually, thankfully, he felt the bitterness creep back. He embraced it, letting it edge out the ache, letting his gaze turn hard and caress her eyes, her sultry mouth, that body he'd once revered. Letting the anger swell until the muscles along his cheeks ticked and his voice deepened like a quarry stripped bare. "You'll have to forgive me, *querida,* if I can't see you as the loyal type."

She flinched back against the wall as if he'd struck her. Her lips parted, then closed. Her eyes looked wounded, flayed. "I'm telling the truth." She turned away and crossed her arms, making the penlight bounce crazily over the stones.

And damned if he didn't feel guilty.

How could she still get to him like this?

"Forget it." He shoved his hand through his hair, rubbed the knotted cords on the back of his neck. There was no point dredging up the past, reliving the pain. It was history; it didn't matter. He'd been over her for years.

And they needed to get out of here fast. "Just get moving," he said.

She chewed her lip, her eyes uncertain in the wobbling light, then glanced behind her at the darkened tunnel. "Through here?"

"There's only one way to go." And the way this night was turning out, it probably led straight to hell.

She turned around and hobbled off. He trailed her, still ducking to keep from knocking his head, his shoulders grazing the jagged walls. He sucked the fetid air through his teeth and exhaled, while the misery of the long night piled up in his mind.

What a fiasco, a total debacle—Antonio's deception, his death. He blinked away that gruesome image. No one, no matter how treacherous, deserved to die that way.

And his own stupidity appalled him. How could he have let his partner fool him? He'd never had a clue that he was being set up.

And then there was Sofia. He clamped his gaze on those satin hips, the seductive sweep of her back. A tumult of emotions swirled through him—bitterness, resentment. Lust.

He hissed out his breath. He'd never met a woman who both infuriated and aroused him.

Especially one he couldn't trust.

And now he was stuck with her, at least until that killer was caught.

Suddenly aware that she was listing oddly, he narrowed his gaze on her legs. She held the penlight in her right hand, clutched the hem of her gown and her shoes in the left.

"What happened to your shoes?" he asked.

"I took them off." She sounded winded, but she didn't stop. "I didn't want to make any noise until I knew for sure who was in the hall."

He grunted. So maybe she hadn't been trying to betray him back there. At least that was something.

But even walking barefoot on the uneven stones wouldn't cause that limp. He studied the awkward way she moved, listened to her breath wheeze. "Are you hurt?"

"I'm fine." Her tight tone contradicted her words.

His frown deepened. What could have happened to her? Then the light swung down, and a shadow gleamed on her calf. His heart thumped. "Wait a minute."

She stopped and braced her hand against the wall. "What?"

"Hand me the light." He grabbed it from her and squatted on his heels. "Turn around and hold up your dress. There's something on your leg."

"Luke, it doesn't matter."

"The hell it doesn't." He aimed the penlight at her leg and his pulse plunged. A raw gash marred her calf and oozed with blood.

He hissed. That had to hurt. "What happened?"

"I got shot."

"Shot?" He yanked his gaze up to hers. "Why didn't you say something?"

She lifted her shoulder in a defeated motion and looked away. He dropped his gaze to the wound again, then angled the light to the dark splotches staining the stones.

He muttered a curse. She was losing too much blood. He had to get her to a doctor, fast. But where could he find one that wouldn't report them to the cops?

He pinched the bridge of his nose. "Look, we need to bandage this and stop the bleeding."

"It's not that bad."

"Bad enough." As raw as that gash looked, he was surprised she could even walk. "And we've got a few minutes. It'll take the guards that long to find the latch."

"You think they know where the door is?"

"They'd have to be blind not to see it." He raised his brows. "You're leaving a nice trail of blood for them to follow, *querida*."

"Oh, God." Her voice quivered, and she placed her hand on her mouth. "I'm so sorry. I never meant to lead them here."

He exhaled, rose and handed back the penlight. And for the first time, he noticed the strain etching her face, the taut grooves bracketing her mouth. She had to be in tremendous pain.

"Look." He gentled his voice. "There's a spot just ahead where the tunnel widens. We can bandage your leg there if you think you can make it that far."

She searched his eyes. "You've been in here before?"

"A few months ago when I was doing a security check." Not that it had done any good. The royal Roma couple had still died.

"I'll make it," she said, and he had to admire her pluck. She was determined, if nothing else.

She limped off again, slower now, and he mulled over this new twist. Why would they shoot Sofia if she'd been involved in the theft?

Unless they'd intended to eliminate her all along. A chill struck his nerves at the thought, but it made sense. With Antonio gone, she was the only one who could prove Luke hadn't stolen that necklace. Worse, she'd seen Paco kill Antonio—which doubled their reasons to want her dead.

Which meant it was up to Luke to protect her—whether she was guilty, believed him about her patron, or not.

A minute later, the tunnel widened slightly. Part of one wall had crumbled, scattering stones and exposing the ancient garderobe, the palace's primitive plumbing chute that dropped to the ground below. The result was an alcove—tiny, but wider than the narrow passage they'd just crept through.

"Stop here," he said. "Let's get that leg wrapped." But they needed to do it fast. They didn't have more than a few minutes' lead on the police.

Sofia paused and turned back to face him, shivered and rubbed her bare arms. He pulled his car key from his pocket, then lifted the hem of her dress.

"What are you doing?" she asked.

"Cutting up your dress. Unless you've got something else we can use for a bandage?"

"No." She sighed. "Go ahead."

He used the key to punch a hole in the satin, then tore off several long strips, while Sofia held the dress up and helped. Then he removed his tuxedo jacket, kicked aside the loose stones and spread it out. "Here, sit on this."

He moved in close to help her. She grabbed his shoulder for balance, and her body curved into his. Her soft, very feminine body. Their eyes met. A sudden tension hovered between them. And they both went perfectly still.

The shadowy light cocooned them, making the embrace seductive, intimate, tempting. His pulse began to batter his skull.

She felt good in his arms. Too good. And it had been so long.

But this was wrong. The wrong woman, the wrong time.

He grasped her waist, felt her heat sear his hand through the satin gown, while his pulse rocked loud in his ears. He helped her to the ground, aware of her soft, lush body molded to his, the weight of her breast brushing his arm, the compelling scent of her skin.

"Thanks," she said, her voice breathy, and he had to force himself to let go.

She tugged the dress above her knee, and he cleared his throat. "Shine the light on your leg." He lowered himself to one knee and pulled his handkerchief from his pocket. "You'll have to help hold this in place."

He bent forward just as she did and, despite his intentions, he paused. She was so close, her face just inches from his, and the urge to tilt up her chin, to slant his lips over hers in a deep, hot kiss nearly did him in.

Instead, he pressed the handkerchief to her calf. Her hand covered his, and desire shuddered through him, a hot jolt scalding his veins.

Their gazes collided again, and memories slashed through him—her feverish lips, her slick, velvet skin. That delirious moment when sanity ceased and their bodies exploded in bliss.

He dropped his gaze to her parted lips, hauled it back up. Their gazes held and he saw the desire in her eyes, the same stunning need he knew she'd see reflected in his.

Damn, she'd been hot. So hot that he'd dreamed of her, fantasized about her, every day for five long years, despite the betrayal and lies.

But this woman was treacherous, unreliable. And no way would he relive the pain she'd dragged him through. No matter how much he craved that exquisite body, he couldn't forget the past.

He ripped his gaze from hers and leaned back. "Hold this in place while I wrap it."

He started wrapping the strip of cloth around her leg, far too conscious of where his hands touched, of the silky gleam of her thigh. And the faint trembling of her hands, the tug of her breath told him she felt that pull, too.

But he forged on, forcing himself to ignore the insistent pulsing in his groin, to concentrate on the problem at hand. "So who shot you?"

She exhaled and the soft sound rent the still air. "I don't know. There was a *guardia civil* there—he tried to arrest me, just like you said—but then Paco drew his gun."

His hands jerked. "The bodyguard was there?" How could she have put herself in danger like that?

"I didn't see him at first. I thought it was don Fernando. But then he pulled out his gun, and I ran. That's when I got shot."

She shivered, her eyes vulnerable again, and he pulled his gaze away. For a moment, neither spoke. "Do you really think you're being framed?" she finally asked.

"It's the only thing that makes sense. Here, hold this." While she held the end of the cloth in place, he picked up another piece and wrapped it on top. "Look, you said Antonio hired you to make that replica."

"So?"

"So if he only wanted to steal the necklace, why go to all this trouble? Why didn't he just swap the replica for the original? I never would have known."

Because no matter what he thought about Sofia, he couldn't deny her talent. She was the foremost restorer of ancient amber, the best in the world. Her passion, her nearly magical ability to understand the living stone had brought her worldwide acclaim.

And she made flawless reproductions, copies nearly as priceless as the originals and coveted by celebrities, museums... Hell, with her skill, even other experts wouldn't have known that necklace was fake—at least not without running tests.

"I would have known what he'd done," she pointed out.

"Not necessarily. You would have assumed that after the ceremony he'd switched the original back. And once the necklace went to Romanistan, you never would have seen it again."

"Maybe." She frowned. "But why would Paco kill Antonio if they were partners?"

He reached for the last strip of cloth. "To eliminate a witness, probably. They want everyone to think I'm guilty. So they can't risk letting someone who knows the truth live."

Even in the dim light, he saw her face pale. "You mean like me?"

"Like both of us, *querida*. We both know the truth." Their gazes held. She raised her hand to her throat.

"Oh, God," she whispered.

Oh, God was right. They were in a hell of a mess.

He pulled his attention back to the bandage, tied a knot to secure it, then rested back on his heels.

She inhaled, a shaky, feeble sound that told him how rattled she really was. "But…the royal family. Who murdered them?"

Good question. "Hard to say. It might have been unrelated. Terrorists maybe."

She frowned. "Because they wanted the necklace?"

"Maybe. Or they wanted to get rid of the king." When the controversial necklace had surfaced in the Spanish bank vault, Spain decided to donate it to Romanistan, the reputed homeland of the Gypsy people. It was a brilliant move, not only lending support to Romanistan's moderate leader and helping stabilize the volatile region, but gaining Spain access to Romanistan's vast reserves of oil.

"A lot of people don't want Romanistan stable," he added. "And eliminating the king could lead to war." Even nuclear war. Which meant there would be a worldwide hunt to get that necklace back.

"I guess it's possible they're unrelated," she said, her voice doubtful. "It would be an awful coincidence, though."

"Yeah." He grimaced, then shook his head. "My gut tells me there's a connection between those murders and the theft. Something more than a simple distraction."

Plus he couldn't shake the feeling that this was somehow personal. A vendetta. But why would don Fernando want to ruin him? Luke had never met the man before working at his estate. So what did he have against him?

He rubbed the dull ache between his brows and fought off a wave of fatigue. He couldn't worry about that now. He had to get them to safety first.

He rose while Sofia pulled on her shoes. He held out his hand, and she grabbed it, and he tugged her to her feet. "How does that feel?"

She put weight on her leg and gasped. "Better."

"Right." He knew better than that. He bent to pick up his jacket. But then a soft clank in the distance broke the stillness.

His pulse skipped, and he slowly straightened. That sound had come from down the tunnel. Someone was at the other end.

"Luke," Sofia whispered.

He motioned with his hand to cut her off. The police had beaten them to the exit. Now what were they going to do?

He searched his memory of the bolt-hole, but there were no side passages branching off, no more secret doors.

They were trapped.

"Through the garderobe—the old plumbing chute," he decided. There wasn't another way out. "Give me the flashlight."

She handed it over, and he knelt and aimed the light down the chute. It was a fifteen foot drop to the ground, barely wide enough to squeeze through. But they didn't have a choice.

"You go first. Sit over here on the edge." Despite everything, he wished he could spare her this. "Hold on to the sleeve of my jacket. I'll lower you down as far as I can. You'll have to drop the rest of the way, though." And land on her injured leg.

She perched on the edge of the chute and chewed her lip. "What's down there?"

"Just dirt."

"Okay." Their eyes held and, despite her fears, he knew she'd try.

He handed her the sleeve of his jacket, set the penlight down and adjusted his position, bracing himself to offset her weight. "Get a good grip, then push off."

Footsteps pounded in the tunnel now. Sofia grabbed the jacket's sleeve and slid off the edge.

He lowered her down the chute, inching the jacket through his burning palms to control her descent, trying to keep her from bumping the walls. His biceps throbbed. The muscles along his back wrenched. Sweat dripped into his eyes, and he blinked away the sting.

Then the jacket played out. "That's it," he said softly. "I can't go any lower. As soon as you hit the ground, move out of the way."

"All right." Her voice quavered in the darkness below him. And then suddenly she let go. The pressure on the jacket eased. He rocked back, and she shrieked.

The sharp cry echoed up the shaft, and his gut clenched. Damn, that must have hurt.

The footsteps behind him grew louder now, drumming toward him with increasing speed. Adrenaline hammered his veins. He couldn't wait any longer. He just hoped she'd rolled out of the way.

He dropped his jacket down the chute and lowered himself over the edge. He balanced on his forearms for a moment, braced his thighs against the sides. Then he grabbed hold of the ledge and began to work his way down. The rough stone grated his palms, shredded his clothes. His shoulders shook with fatigue.

Then footsteps pounded above him and a bright light flashed on his face.

"Policía," a man yelled. "Stop, or I'll shoot."

Damn. Maybe that necklace really was cursed.

He sucked in his breath and let go.

Chapter 4

The gunshot ricocheted down the garderobe, thundering off the rock walls, echoing through Luke's skull as he plunged toward earth. He crashed into the ground, then rolled, ignoring the spasm jolting his legs from the brutal impact. Rocks gouged his shoulders, his back, but he forced himself to keep rolling to get out of the line of fire.

Sofia's body stopped him.

His heart fisted, then dove, and he shoved himself to his knees. Why wasn't she moving? Was she hurt? "Sofia. Sofia!"

He shook her shoulder, but she didn't respond. He shook it again, harder, and his pulse raced into his throat. "Sofia. *Di algo*. Are you okay?"

Her eyelids fluttered open, and he hissed out air. Thank God, she was alive. Because for a moment there...

"I'm fine. I—" She winced, then moaned. "My leg."

He could imagine. That jackknife landing would have

been agony on her gunshot wound. But they couldn't linger here and assess the damage. The police would arrive at any time.

Swearing softly, he speared his hand through his hair. "We've got to keep going. Can you stand?"

"Just give me a second." She rolled forward and struggled to her knees.

"Here. Hold on to me." He crouched and put his arm around her waist to lift her. His hand touched bare flesh, and she flinched.

He jerked. "What?"

"I…I just scraped my side, that's all."

He didn't doubt it. The stones had shredded her elegant dress, peeling it into strips. He could imagine the damage to her skin.

More gently now, he adjusted his hold on her waist and tugged her to her feet. She leaned against him, panting, one hand clutching his shirt, her soft breath caressing his ear. Strands of loose hair fell around her face, tumbling from the lopsided twist.

"Can you walk?"

"Yes, I'm—" she stepped forward, gasped, and he grabbed her again, afraid that she would pass out "—fine." She sucked in her breath. "Really. I'm okay."

She was lying. Pain tightened the corners of her eyes and etched lines around her mouth. But there wasn't anything he could do about that now. He dropped his hands and stepped back.

"Which way now?" she asked.

Good question. He glanced around. They'd landed where the garderobe drained, outside the palace on a rocky slope. In fact, considering how steep the hill was, they were lucky they hadn't rolled down.

Then again, it might have been better if they had.

As it was, they stood highlighted against the wall, trapped by the spotlights that ringed the palace, as visible as actors on a brightly lit stage. But if they moved away from the wall to escape the spotlights, they'd be seen by the guards on the roof. Guards he had put in place.

"The easiest way out is toward the front," he said, keeping his voice low. "But the entrance will be crawling with police."

"Down the hill then?"

He glanced at the shallow trench leading into the darkness. "Too obvious. This is the first place they'll look. We need to do something they won't expect."

Like climb down the other side. His mind flashed to the sheer slope that backed the palace. Could Sofia make it? Could he? Did they have a choice?

"Back here. Come on." His sense of urgency rising, he scooped his tuxedo jacket from the ground and slipped it on. The dark color would help him blend with the night. "Stay close to the wall."

"But shouldn't we get out of the light?"

"Not yet. The guards on the roof could pick us off."

Ignoring her quick intake of breath, he turned and led the way over the slanted ground toward the back of the palace. In the distance, a siren wailed. A second later another joined it, their off-key notes dueling in the summer night.

The hunt was on.

And that's exactly what this was, a manhunt. Anger knifed through him, like talons clawing his gut. They'd set him up tonight. Chosen him. Baited and trapped him like some weak, defenseless prey.

And now they intended to kill him.

They could think again.

He curled his hands, thinned his lips, felt the muscles

bunch in his jaw. They'd played him for a fool, flayed his pride. But he was a survivor. He'd battled his way out of the ghetto, scrapped for every crumb he'd had.

And he would fight this war to win.

His stride lengthening, he closed the distance to the end of the palace, turned the corner and stopped. The light hazed over the rock-strewn ground to the point where the slope dropped off. If they made it past the edge, no one would see them. But then they'd still have to climb down the cliff.

Sofia limped up beside him and stopped. "You want to go down this?" Her voice rose. "Is there even a path?"

His gaze met hers, and he shook his head. "It's not as steep as it looks. We'll stay to the side where the bushes are."

She gnawed her lip. Her eyes stayed frozen on his. Then she jerked her gaze to the cliff.

"They'll have the other routes blocked. There isn't another way."

"I know."

He knew she was scared. He didn't blame her. The descent would be tough in the dark.

But then she lifted her eyes to his. "So who goes first?"

And without warning, a sliver of warmth stole into his chest. She'd been shot, chased, injured, scraped—but she was still willing to climb down that cliff.

Oh, hell. He yanked his gaze away. He didn't want to admire her. He didn't even want to like her. And he sure didn't want to feel that connection to her again, that link.

The physical attraction was bad enough. But he could handle that. He could keep those feelings cornered, contained, battened safely in a distant place.

But that fusing of minds, that need… Never again. No way.

Furious at himself, he wrenched his mind back to the cliff. "I'll go first." The words came out harsh, and she blinked.

"Wait until I've started down, then run to get past the light. And try not to make any noise. We don't want to attract the guards."

Someone shouted from the rooftop then. The sirens grew closer, then cut off abruptly. His body tensed. They had to do this now. "Ready?"

"Yes."

"Then let's go." His adrenaline surging, he crouched and sprinted to the edge of the cliff. Then he slowed, grabbed a bush for balance, picked out a path, and stepped off. Stones slid beneath his feet, but he kept moving, dropping from one foothold to the next, lowering himself away from the edge. When he'd passed safely beyond the light, he stopped.

His breath sawed the air. His pulse drummed a ragged beat. He'd made it. Now it was Sofia's turn.

He watched her as she hurried toward him, doubled over and limping badly, anxiety and pain carved on her face. She slowed and gripped the same bush he had, pivoted to start down. But then her injured leg buckled. She stumbled toward him and gasped. His heart thudding, he leaned forward to block her fall.

"Easy," he murmured as she thumped against him. Pebbles slid loose and bounced around them, and he struggled to keep them from plunging down.

"I'm all right," she whispered when she'd found her balance. But her back was rigid, and she was pulling out the roots on that bush.

And that sliver of admiration, that traitorous warmth around his heart, increased.

He eased his hands from the cliff, keeping his motions slow to calm her. "Okay," he said. "I'm going down now. Watch me and step where I do."

"But I can't see."

"Don't look at the lights. Let your eyes get used to the

darkness." A trick he'd learned as a kid, stealing through the night. "Better?"

"Yes," she whispered, but her breath hitched.

"Good. Now follow me. Take your time. Don't rush, even if you hear any noise."

Hoping she wouldn't hurry and fall—especially if those guards gave chase— he reached for another branch. He tugged it to make sure it would hold his weight and scooted down the hill a few more steps. He glanced back, relieved to see that she'd followed, then returned his attention to the cliff.

He stuck to the safest route, choosing caution over speed for Sofia's sake. But while his progress down the hill was slow, questions about the night careened through his mind. Who shot the royal Roma couple? Were the killings related to the theft? And why steal the necklace tonight when the entire world was watching?

The news would create a media frenzy, no doubt—royals murdered, priceless treasure stolen, Romanistan pushed to the brink of war. And as if that weren't sensational enough, there was the curse.

He grimaced, skirted a boulder and grappled for another handhold. Of course, the curse was nonsense.

But there was one fact he couldn't deny—he'd been involved in this mess for a reason. What that reason was, he didn't know. He'd have to unravel that once they were safe.

He inched around another section of rock, then realized he could make out shadows beneath him. They'd nearly reached the bottom. Now they just had to get up the opposite hill and they'd be on the open road.

He turned back, intending to tell Sofia, but a small stone bounced past his face. He glanced up, blinked as dirt rained onto his head. Sofia let out a muffled cry.

She hurtled toward him, and his lungs froze. He reached out to try to block her, but her momentum knocked him back. He grunted, fell—Sofia with him—into the empty space.

He flailed, unable to latch onto anything, then slammed to the rocky earth. His shoulder and back took the impact, but he didn't slow. Instead, he skidded downward, crashing through bushes, knocking more stones loose, grabbing at anything he could.

He finally smacked against a boulder and stopped. Sofia rammed into him a moment after, knocking the wind from his lungs. He wheezed and bit off a groan.

For several heartbeats, neither moved. Sofia moaned and clutched her head. "Luke, are you all right?"

"Yeah." Although his back ached, and his shoulder burned. He blinked the dirt from his eyes and rolled to his knees. A wave of dizziness made him suck in his breath.

Still dragging at air, he stumbled to his feet and rotated his bruised shoulder to test it. Then he reached down to help Sofia up.

But then a bright light slashed the sky, and his breath stopped. Searchlights. Oh, hell. Just what they didn't need.

"Come on," he urged her. "*¡Rápido!*" His pain forgotten, he grabbed Sofia's hand and yanked her to her feet. Then he hauled her up the short, steep hill, dragging her, not giving her time to slow down. "Faster. Faster!" The guards would see them at any time.

Shouts came from the palace behind them. The searchlight skipped past, barely missing them as it swept the ravine.

Knowing every second counted, Luke ran flat-out, pulling Sofia harder. His thighs burned. His lungs heaved. But they were exposed now, out in the open. They had to take cover fast.

They crested the hill, and he glanced around wildly,

searching for a safe place to hide. But then a deep thrumming sound filled his ears. Vibrations drummed the ground beneath him, and he jerked his gaze to the sky.

His heart stopped. A police helicopter. Could their luck get any worse?

Still towing Sofia, he sprinted across the road toward some bushes while his desperation surged. The rotors pulsed louder, closer. The air around them throbbed.

"In here," he shouted to Sofia, but the deafening noise swallowed his voice. He dropped her arm and shoved through the dense, prickly branches. Thorns snagged his sleeves, clawed his face, but he lunged past them, battling them out of the way to help her crawl inside.

Then he dragged her to the ground. He wrapped his arms around her and pulled her close, ignoring the sharp twigs poking his back.

"My hair," she said, and he saw the problem—her blond hair wouldn't blend in. But she tugged the hem of her gown from beneath her legs, and he helped drape it over her head.

Then suddenly, a bright light flashed. And the helicopter thundered above them like an airborne train, its roar deafening, its searchlight probing. The earth around him shook, jarring his bones, vibrating his teeth.

He huddled against Sofia, sheltering her as the downdraft spun the dirt loose, dislodging stones and leaves. The branches around them swayed, and he couldn't breathe, afraid the bushes would part and reveal them. The intense light lingered, skipped past, flared again.

And then, mercifully, it headed away.

"Don't move yet," he said into Sofia's ear.

Still curled against him, her face buried in his chest, she shook her head. She clung to him, trembling wildly, her soft body plastered to his. His own stomach churning, he held her, absorbing her fear, listening as the thump of the rotors receded, replaced by sirens again.

He finally blew out his breath and slumped back. That had been close. Too close. Sofia eased her hold on his jacket and lifted her head.

"Oh, God, Luke. I'm so sorry. That was all my fault. My leg gave way and I slipped and the stones made noise and—"

"Shh." He put his fingers to her lips. Her eyes were huge in the darkness. Her soft mouth quivered against his hand. Tears streaked her face, forging a trail through the grime to her chin.

She looked exhausted. Dazed. And so beautiful she made his lungs hurt.

He slid his hand up her back to her neck and rested his forehead on hers. Her warm breath hitched and brushed his face. "Luke," she said, her voice cracking.

"Hold on. Just a little longer. Just until we get somewhere safe."

He ran his thumb along her jaw and stroked her neck. He pressed his other hand to her back, feeling the heat of her skin, the violent shivers still jerking through her.

A few heartbeats later, she lifted her chin. Her lips were inches from his, whipping his nerves into sudden awareness. He wanted to kiss her. He wanted to slide his mouth down that skin, taste the heat of her flesh, lose himself in that hot rush of lust.

But he couldn't go there. She needed comfort, not sex. She was injured, shocked, rattled by the harrowing night.

He forced his hands to her shoulders and inched back, increasing the distance between them. Her gaze stayed on his, trapping him, reeling him in, while the blood rocked hard in his ears.

"What are we going to do now?" she whispered.

Get away from temptation, first off. He let go of her shoulders, grabbed a branch above him, and rose. "Get out of here before that helicopter comes back. Find a place to rest." Somewhere they could make plans, get medical help for her leg.

Somewhere the police wouldn't find them.

A sense of inevitability swept through him. He knew only one place that fit that description—aside from the slums where he'd grown up.

El Aro. The Gypsy enclave in downtown Madrid where his aunt Carmen lived.

Grim now, galled at having to ask his relatives for help but knowing he didn't have much choice, he shoved his way out of the shrub. "Come on." He turned back and pulled her out. "We need to find a car."

"Where's yours?"

"Back at the palace." Surrounded by police, no doubt.

Still scanning the area, alert in case the helicopter swung back, he headed toward the parked cars lining the road. Sofia hobbled behind him, not even protesting his intentions, and he wondered if she had grown numb.

He finally spotted an ancient Seat, a car he could quickly hot-wire. He stopped, glanced around to make sure the road was still deserted, and expertly shimmied the lock.

"Get in," he told her.

While she limped around the battered car, he rummaged under the dashboard. He found the ignition wire, isolated the starter, made a few twists and slid inside. A quick touch of the starter wire fired up the engine. Sofia shut her door, and he eased out the clutch and drove off.

The irony of his actions struck him hard. He'd gone full circle in the past few hours, from being poised on the edge of triumph to reverting to a life of crime.

Breaking the vow he'd kept for fifteen years.

He blew out his breath. Fatigue from the long night rocked through him, and he rubbed the ache at the base of his skull. He hadn't asked for this trouble. He'd been set up, sucked in—and now he couldn't escape. He had to find that necklace, clear his name and protect Sofia from Antonio's killer, whether she was involved in this plot or not.

So while he hadn't chosen this war, he couldn't shirk it. He had to fight it with everything he had.

He glanced at Sofia. Her eyes were closed, her breathing rough. Her hair was wrecked, her soft cheeks streaked with grime, her once-elegant gown destroyed. And before he could stop it, something shifted inside him, something long-buried flickered to life.

Maybe it was the weariness, the ordeal of the past hours creeping in, blunting the bitterness he'd harbored for years. Making him remember the good parts—her gentleness, her passion, the sex.

Too dangerous. He yanked his gaze back to the road. This woman had betrayed him. He didn't dare trust her, no matter how innocent she looked right now. Plus he had police on his tail, a killer stalking his heels. He couldn't let down his guard.

Because if he wasn't careful, he'd fall for Sofia again. And that would be the biggest danger of all.

Chapter 5

The dull pounding in Sofia's skull and the savage burn torching her leg dragged her to awareness. She lifted her hand, pressed her trembling fingers to her forehead to still the wild ache slicing her brain and moaned. But she couldn't block the images flashing through her mind—that pooling blood, the splattered flesh, Antonio's bulging, terrified eyes. Nausea churned from her belly, swelled into her throat. What an exhausting, horrendous night.

She'd fallen into a nightmare, had her safe, calm world stripped away. Now if she could only wake up.

"Are you all right?" Luke asked, his deep voice rumbling over the drone of the car's engine.

She drew in her breath, cracked opened her eyes and focused her blurry gaze on him. He frowned out the windshield at the road, the hard planes of his profile grim, his beard stubble dark, pronounced. His short black hair was mussed, and dirt streaked from his temple to his jaw. He looked ruthless, lethal, and the sheer maleness of him made her heart thump.

"Alive, anyway." Thanks to him. Although she couldn't remember ever feeling this wretched. Every part of her had been scraped, wrenched, pummeled, and shot into a throbbing mass of misery. "How about you?"

"I'll survive." His gaze met hers, his eyes unreadable in the dim light, and her heart raced even more.

She jerked her gaze to the street, blinked to get her bearings. A strangely curving, four-story apartment building loomed ahead. "Where are we?"

"Moratalaz. El Aro."

El Aro. She'd heard of the low-income project. She leaned forward, frowned at the smattering of broken windows, the trash blowing across the sidewalk, the roughly patched cement walls. "Who lives here?"

"My aunt Carmen. We'll rest at her house tonight." He pulled into a crowded parking lot, and she scanned the clotheslines stretched across balconies, the crates and wooden pallets stacked against the walls. Deep, male voices spilled from ground-level bars.

"Do you think it's safe?"

"For now." His gaze met hers again. "The police don't usually get involved with the Gypsies. Not if they can help it. We can hide out here for a while."

"I see." She rubbed the ache pulsing between her brows, the exhaustion lashing her eyes. She'd never felt so off-kilter, so lost. The night's events had flung her completely off-balance. She'd had to flee a killer, the police, steal a car...

Fear bubbled inside her. She'd never committed a crime before.

Unlike Luke. He'd hot-wired this car like a pro.

She slid another glance at his profile—the dusky skin and hollowed cheekbones, the masculine slant of his jaw. The pounding in her head ramped up, and she drew in a shaky breath. She didn't know what to think about Luke. He'd protected her, kept her safe, and yet she knew so little about him. In the months they'd spent at don Fernando's estate, he'd never mentioned he had family in Madrid—or that he had a criminal background. She'd only found that out when don Fernando's gems had disappeared from his vault.

The vault Luke had been hired to secure.

And now… She blew out her breath, unable to think past the fatigue bludgeoning her brain. The entire night was too bizarre. She desperately needed to sleep, to make this ordeal disappear for a while. Maybe then it would all make sense.

Luke downshifted again, then double-parked in front of the high-rise building. He set the brake but left the motor running. "Wait here."

He opened his door and climbed out, then raked her with his eyes. "Here." He took off his tuxedo jacket and tossed it back in. "Put this on."

Grateful, she grabbed the jacket and slung it over her tattered dress. The jacket was covered with dirt and smelled of Luke, and she hugged it close, relishing even that small comfort in her upended world.

Luke strode around the car to the apartment building, and she kept her gaze glued to him like a lifeline, pulling the jacket tighter around her. He pressed the intercom at the door, braced one muscled forearm against the wall, planted his other hand low on his hip. The motion tightened his shirt against his back, highlighting his powerful shoulders and neck.

Her heart drummed. He looked tough, virile enough to

defeat the world. And no matter what else had happened during the past five years, his appeal hadn't diminished one bit.

A second later, he lifted his head. He spoke into the intercom, then loped back to the car and motioned for her to get out.

Moving awkwardly, trying not to jostle her injured leg, she pushed her door open and slid out. Luke took her arm and helped her up, but fire bolted up her calf and she groaned.

"Easy. Hold on to me." He slid his hand around her waist, and she clung to him as she hobbled across the sidewalk to the door. And despite the pain searing her leg, the fatigue mauling her head, she was conscious of his big hand splayed beneath her breast, the press of his leg against hers.

He paused at the door and pushed the intercom button again, while she struggled to catch her breath.

"*¿Sí?*" a woman's voice scratched through the speaker.

"*Soy yo.*" The door buzzed, and Luke pushed it open. "Come on."

Still clutching his arm, she limped with him into the lobby. The door closed behind them, blocking out the noise from the street. "Will your aunt mind us showing up like this?" she asked in the sudden hush. "It's the middle of the night."

"Don't worry. She'll be fine."

Doubtful, but too tired to argue the point, she hobbled across the tiled foyer to the waiting elevator. They stepped inside, and she grabbed the bar along the back while Luke leaned forward and punched the buttons. The doors slid closed, and the elevator cage creaked up.

She swayed, tightened her grip on the railing, and shifted her gaze to Luke. He faced forward, as if mesmerized by the numbers of the floors they passed, and for the first time that night she indulged herself, letting her gaze linger on the slant of his shadowed cheeks, the dark scruff coating his jaw, the cords of his muscled throat. His primal masculinity jolted through her again, making her pulse speed up, heating her blood.

She cased out her breath. It had always been like this. From the moment she'd seen him at don Fernando's estate, everything about this man had enthralled her—his lethal looks, his outrageous talent, the intensity in his eyes.

He turned his head then, and that hot gaze collided with hers.

Her heartbeat faltered, skipped, then zigzagged through her chest like a frenzied hare. She dragged at air, saw his eyes darken as the look lengthened, trapping her, sucking her in. And she couldn't look away.

Or stop the erotic memories scorching through her. His urgent kiss. Those callused hands. The way his breath rasped and muscles bunched, rippling and straining beneath his skin.

She saw desire heat his eyes, the need in the way his jaw flexed, and knew he remembered it, too. But he was fighting the attraction, she realized. He didn't *want* to want her.

Hurt mushroomed through her, and she jerked her gaze away. The elevator jolted to a stop, and she clutched the rail, grateful for the distraction. She kept her gaze averted as the doors creaked open, ignored the feel of him gripping her waist. She concentrated on maneuvering down the hall, beating back the disappointment flaying her gut.

She couldn't worry about Luke right now. And she couldn't dwell on the past. She had to rest, sort through the evening's disaster, figure out how to solve this mess.

And she would solve it. No matter what it took, she had to get her life back. She'd worked too hard, too long, to let it fall apart now.

"Hola, tía," Luke called out as they entered his aunt's apartment. He let go of her waist and shut the door, and a squat, thick woman in a bathrobe and slippers shuffled into

the hall. Her face was dark, leathered like that of a wizened tortoise, her waist-long braid shot with gray. Her gaze arrowed straight to Sofia, then swept her with disdain.

Sofia's stomach plunged. So much for a warm welcome. And how often had she felt that in her life?

She hung back and clutched Luke's jacket more closely around her as the woman's gaze shifted to Luke. He strode forward, stooped and kissed her on each cheek, and they greeted each other in Spanish. No, she decided, Spanish and something else. The Gypsy language Caló?

Whatever it was, his aunt clearly didn't want her here. The woman gestured wildly, her voice low and harsh, and scowled in her direction. *"Nos trae mal fario. Maldita paya,"* she muttered and stomped away.

Paya, the word they gave to non-Gypsies. The churning in her stomach grew.

Luke turned back to help her, his eyebrows lowered, but she motioned him away. "I'm okay." She struggled to keep her tone light, dredge up a smile, assume an expression of confidence she didn't quite feel.

"Really," she added. "Go on and talk to your aunt."

He strode off, and she followed the hall to the living room, battling back that familiar knot of nerves and shame, the painful barrage of memories—never being wanted, never belonging, never knowing what to say or do.

A tight ache clutched at her throat, and she locked her gaze on the television in the corner, determined not to succumb to the past. She focused on the torn vinyl sofa, the pictures of saints tacked to the cracking walls, the plants crowding the tiny room. Trying to block out the sound of Luke arguing with his aunt in the kitchen. Over her.

They'd always argued before they'd kicked her out.

She twisted a strand of her hair, rubbed her arms, willed

the memories away. She didn't need this. Not now. Not here. Hadn't the night been bad enough?

Luke emerged from the kitchen a second later and scowled in her direction. "Wait here," he said, then disappeared down a hall.

The aunt came out next and gave her a level stare. Sofia pasted a smile on her face, lifted her chin, struggled to act calm, in control. Her lips quivered, and she pressed them together hard.

The aunt made a sound of disgust and followed Luke. Sofia swayed on her feet, blinking back the misery, the exhaustion, wanting desperately to curl up and fall asleep, to let the entire night be merely a nightmare, to wake up to the security of her workshop, her precious amber, to lose herself in the beautiful stones.

But then Luke strode back. He'd changed into jeans, a black T-shirt, dark tennis shoes. His hair was damp, as if he'd splashed water on his face, and a stray drop slid down his whiskered jaw.

"I'm going to go ditch the car," he said. "It might take me awhile."

Her stomach lurched, and panic drummed. "I'll come with you." She didn't want to be left alone here.

His frown deepened. "No, you stay here and rest your leg."

"I'm fine. Really. I don't need to rest."

"The hell you don't. You're dead on your feet."

"But your aunt doesn't want me here. She—"

"She'll do what she has to. And she knows how to care for that wound." He moved close and cupped her chin. His thumb stroked her cheek. His callused skin raised shivers on her arms. And his dark gold eyes stayed on hers. "I need to move fast, *querida*. It's safer for me without you."

Her lips quivered again, and she pulled in a reedy breath. He was right, of course. She would only slow him down.

Then his aunt returned, and he lowered his hand. Sofia hugged her arms at the loss.

Still scowling, the aunt thrust a stack of clothes, a towel and a box of hair dye into her hands.

"Hair dye?" She jerked her gaze to Luke's. "I don't think—"

"We can't afford to attract attention. And there aren't many blondes around here."

She swallowed, nodded. "Right. You're right." She was a fugitive. On the run. Her world tilted even more.

"Ven acá," the aunt ordered and motioned for Sofia to follow her down the hall.

Sofia looked at Luke, her throat thick, a sudden fear spiraling through her. What if something happened to him? What if he got arrested? What if he didn't come back?

"Luke." Her voice cracked, and she dragged in her breath. "Be careful."

"Always, *querida.*" A cynical smile edged his mouth. "I'm used to looking out for myself."

So was she.

And that was what she was afraid of.

He strode away. The front door closed. And she felt bereft, abandoned, alone.

She'd fallen into a nightmare, all right. But instead of ending, it just kept getting worse.

Luke's aunt was a tyrant, Sofia discovered. Once Luke left, she turned into a whirlwind of activity, cutting and dying Sofia's hair, cleaning and bandaging her wound, making sure Sofia showered, downed painkillers and antibiotics— all while badgering her in a nonstop torrent of fiery Spanish.

Sofia had finally collapsed on the sofa in her borrowed

clothes, barely able to prop her eyes open, when Luke strode back through the door. Their gazes met, and he halted across the room. His eyes swept her face, her too-tight jeans and T-shirt, the tennis shoes on her feet. Her heart began to batter her chest.

"So what do you think?" she asked, suddenly breathless. "Do I look different enough?"

He grunted and muttered something she couldn't catch. Not sure what that meant, she tugged at her wisps of dark hair. "Did you get rid of the car?"

"Yeah. I left it in Fuencarral." He crossed the room, grabbed the remote from atop the television set, flipped through the channels to the morning news. "With any luck, they won't find it for a day or two." He tossed the remote onto the coffee table. "You want something to drink?"

"No, thanks." She stifled a yawn while he strode to the kitchen and returned with a glass.

He pulled a bottle of cognac from the corner cabinet, splashed some into his glass, and then stared out the balcony window, his hard body backlit by the rising sun. Sofia tried to concentrate on the news, but everything about Luke drew her—the edgy darkness in his face, the intensity in his eyes, the raw tension in his muscled frame.

"So what's our plan?" she asked to distract herself.

He glanced at her, then moved to the armchair nearest the couch and sat. "We'll rest here for a few hours. You can sleep in my old room. I'll take the couch."

"You used to live here?"

"Briefly." He took a slug of cognac, cradled the glass in his big hands. And she was struck again by how little she knew of this man. She'd adored him—revered him—during their brief but torrid affair. And she'd been convinced that they were soul mates, both loners, two kindred spirits who'd used their unusual skills to survive.

But unlike her, Luke had a home, an aunt. But he'd never told her that. Apparently, he hadn't cared about her enough to share his past.

His eyes met hers. "I stayed here after I'd been arrested, released on parole. My aunt took me in."

"Oh." She wondered what to say to that. "That was… nice of her."

"Right." He let out a bitter laugh. "It would have been nicer if she'd taken me from El Salobral."

El Salobral. The shanty-filled encampment on the edge of Madrid. She'd passed it on her trips into town.

He drained the cognac in his glass, as she watched the muscles in his throat work, his Adam's apple dip. And she wondered about the rest of it. Why he'd become a thief. Why he'd left this aunt who loved him. What had made him so bitter about the past.

But this wasn't the place, the moment, to ask.

Suddenly, he lunged forward and grabbed the remote. He cranked up the volume on the television set, his gaze glued to the screen.

"What?" she asked, but he signaled for her to be quiet. She perched on the edge of the sofa and watched the screen, listening to the newscaster, trying to catch everything he said.

He was discussing the theft, the curse. Pictures of the palace flashed across the screen, close-ups of police vans, ambulances, dead bodies being carted away on stretchers, the surviving princess looking distraught. Sofia's heart plunged, and the horror rolled through her again—Antonio, the dead Roma king and queen. She hugged her arms and rocked, wanting the violence to disappear, feeling the terror surge, the horror build again in her throat.

And then her photo appeared alongside Luke's, and her breath caught. She was being blamed. They both were.

She gaped at the television, stunned, numb, as if a bomb had detonated her world. The police suspected them—she'd known that. But it seemed so much worse to see their pictures plastered across the screen, to know that the entire world now blamed them.

The significance of that crashed through her and jarred the breath from her lungs. She didn't just need to clear her name with the local police anymore. Her life had been destroyed— her reputation, her acceptance in the antiquities world. She was a pariah. No museum, no collector would trust a woman accused of murder and theft.

And without her career, her art, she had no home, no acceptance. She had nothing. Everything she'd worked for, longed for, was gone.

Her stomach pitched, and her throat closed up. She struggled to suck in a breath. "But how can they think we did this? We didn't do anything wrong!"

"You think they care?" His voice was bitter, raw, and her gaze met his. She saw the rage in his eyes, the pain.

And suddenly she knew. He hadn't stolen those gems five years back. He'd been innocent, wrongly accused, just as they both were now. And no one had believed him. No one had stood up for him. Not even her.

Oh, God. What had she done?

Her stomach wrenched. Shame and regret seared through her. She eyed the rigid line of his jaw, the unyielding planes of his face, the anger that masked his deep pain.

Pain she'd caused. She'd turned against him back then, sided with don Fernando. No wonder he despised her now.

A noise from the kitchen drew her attention. Stricken, she dragged her gaze to his aunt. The woman glared at her from the doorway, her condemnation plain.

Sofia looked away, her guilt crushing, overwhelming. She

understood his aunt's hostility now. And frankly, she couldn't blame her. She probably thought Sofia had framed Luke in the past—and was responsible for this trouble now.

Luke rose and prowled to the cabinet, then took out a bottle and refilled his glass. His aunt said something sharp, and he hissed in answer, then knocked the liquid back.

Sofia dropped her head in her trembling hands, her misery complete. Talk about a nightmare! She'd lost everything tonight. Her security, her career—the most important part of her life. She was being pursued by a killer, hunted by the police.

But all that paled compared to the harm she'd done to Luke. She'd made an appalling, horrendous mistake.

"Luke, I…" His gaze burned into hers. A huge lump wedged in her throat, and she shook her head, unable to speak.

He exhaled and set down his glass. "Come on. I'll show you to your room. We'll talk after we've had some sleep."

She nodded, rose, hobbled behind him down the hall. She felt shredded, devastated, perilously close to breaking apart.

She'd been wrong, so wrong. And it was too late to change the past, to repair the damage she'd done.

But she knew one thing. She owed this man an apology. And she needed to make it now.

Chapter 6

Sofia limped behind Luke into a tiny bedroom off the hallway, her steps dragging, the thick weight of remorse sinking her chest. She doubted he would make this easy; the grim line of his mouth, the tight set to his jaw told her that he was too angry, too hostile to listen to her after all these years. But she had to make him hear her, before she lost her nerve.

He flicked on the overhead light, then strode to the window and pulled down the metal slats. The heavy blinds muffled the noise of traffic from the street below and blocked the rising sun. He headed back across the room, and she inhaled, gathered her courage. "Luke," she began.

"Yeah?" He paused at the door, and his gaze met hers.

Anxiety clutched at her lungs. How on earth to start? "I know this is late, and it's no excuse, but I just wanted to tell you…that I'm sorry. That I didn't believe you back then."

He stiffened. The dark, stubbled planes of his face went still, and she feared he was shutting her out.

"I still don't know what happened. It doesn't make any sense, but I didn't know—you'd never told me…" She stopped, sucked in another breath, knowing she was muddling this up. "The police said you'd used me to get those gems that night. And I felt like such a fool because I thought…"

She'd thought he'd loved her, truly loved her. And his deception had ripped her apart.

The knot in her throat swelled tight, and she choked it back, hoping he'd say something, anything. But he just stood there, his face frozen, his eyes defensive, as if he'd thrown up a shield and walled her out.

Not that she blamed him after the damage she'd done.

"I know it doesn't change anything, but I just wanted you to know." She lifted her hand in a futile gesture, let it drop. "I never meant to hurt you."

He still didn't react, just stared at her. And the misery of the night seeped through her, thickening her chest, killing her hopes.

"I'm sorry," she whispered, and her throat clammed shut. "I really am." Tears burned in her eyes, and she blinked to keep them back.

He closed his eyes then, and tipped back his head. The tendons along his throat worked. The muscles in his whiskered jaw flexed.

Then he exhaled roughly, opened his eyes, and locked his gaze on hers. And for an eternity he just looked at her, his eyes guarded, skeptical. And the weight of the past five years hung between them, years of hurt and doubt, anger and blame.

And she realized just how much damage she'd done.

Her stomach plunged. She swayed, swamped with the

need to touch him, hug him, to beg him to forgive her and forget the past.

She'd loved this man. Oh, how she'd loved this man. And she'd given him everything—her heart, her body.

But not her trust.

She rubbed her arms, clamped down her trembling lips, needing to tell him why, to somehow explain. "Luke," she pleaded, her voice raw. But hot tears welled, and she couldn't speak.

"Oh, hell. Don't cry." He stepped forward and cupped her jaw with his hand. He tugged her chin up, and her gaze met his, her vision blurry with tears.

And all she could do was look at him, knowing there was nothing she could say, nothing she could do, no way to change the painful past.

He caressed her cheek with his callused thumb, brushed a stray tear away. The movement was gentle, tender. More than she deserved. More tears brimmed, and she battled them back.

His thumb slowed, faltered, stopped. His gaze roamed from her eyes to her lips. And then he frowned, as if perplexed. Her heart skipped, then sprinted hard.

And then he lowered his head and touched his lips to hers, and her heart nearly jumped from her chest. His mouth moved deliberately over hers, the kiss reassuring, soothing.

He shifted closer, fitted his big, hard body to hers, and she inhaled his warmth, his scent. Desire crept through her, the urge to stroke him, caress the hollows of his face, absorb his power, his strength, his heat.

He lifted his mouth from hers but didn't move. His gaze singed her lips. His breath fanned her face. Her heart looped and stuttered through her chest.

And memories sizzled through her. The rasp of his voice. The hot, slow slide of his mouth.

He made a low, rough sound and jerked her close. And he slanted his mouth across hers, kissing her for real this time, hauling her into his arms, plundering her mouth.

The kiss was carnal, deep, raw. *Devastating.* Her senses whirled. Her knees turned weak. Her pulse went wild in her veins.

He shoved his hand through her hair, trapping her head. He cradled her jaw and devoured her mouth. The kiss was rough, relentless, exactly the way she'd remembered, the way she'd craved. And his urgency set her ablaze.

But just as suddenly, he pulled away.

She gasped, fought to keep her balance as he stepped back. "You're exhausted." His voice was hoarse, his expression dangerous. "Get some rest." He turned and strode away.

Her heart thundered as the door clicked closed. What had happened? Why had he kissed her like that? And why on earth had he stopped?

Reeling, her body shaking from the need he'd provoked, she stumbled to the bed. Then she sank to the mattress, curled her knees, and rocked. Her head pounded. Emotions churned through her belly—arousal, frustration, remorse.

What a strange and miserable night. She'd witnessed murders, fled the police. And Luke…that kiss. She closed her eyes and shivered hard.

He was as lethal as she remembered. Rough. Hot. Perfect. That kiss had blown her apart.

She dragged in her breath, dabbed her eyes on her sleeve, struggled to pull herself back from the lust, to make some sense of it all. How could she have misjudged him back then? How could she have been so wrong?

The evidence had pointed to Luke. He'd had a juvenile record. He'd installed the security at the estate, so he'd known how everything worked. She'd shown him the restorations she'd done, the cache of ancient jewels, so he'd seen what they had in the vault. And he'd made mind-blanking, soul-shattering love to her in her room that night—and then disappeared before dawn.

But if he hadn't taken those gems, who had? Could don Fernando have lied? Why would he? He'd had nothing to gain by those thefts. He'd even donated the insurance money to a museum in Madrid.

She rubbed the ache hammering her temples. There had to be another explanation, one that didn't involve either man. And somehow she had to find it—plus help solve their current mess.

But not now. Now she needed to sleep, to forget the dreadful night. She was so tired, so strung out emotionally that she wanted to retch.

She sat up and tugged at her borrowed T-shirt. Her gaze landed on the telephone on the bedside table, and she paused with her hand on her sleeve. She still had to warn don Fernando about his bodyguard, Paco. He'd be in danger until he knew.

A deep sense of unease trickled through her, and she flicked her gaze to the door. Luke wouldn't want her to call him. He didn't trust the man.

What if Luke was right? What if she *was* wrong? Could don Fernando be working with Paco, as Luke believed?

No. That was ridiculous. Don Fernando protected antiquities, he didn't steal them. He was a generous, honest man—the man who'd taken her in, paid for her education, treated her like the daughter he'd never had.

And she'd made a mistake before—abandoning Luke when he needed her most. She couldn't do the same to her patron now. Plus, don Fernando could help them. He had contacts, connections.

She bit her lip, wavered, then reached for the phone. Five years ago, she'd sat by and done nothing while Luke was blamed. Her fears, her insecurities, had caused her to side against him. And while she couldn't change the past, she could do something now.

Calling don Fernando was a good place to start.

He was losing control.

Luke turned his aunt's car onto a narrow side street in the old part of Madrid that afternoon, still kicking himself for his behavior. Touching Sofia had been a mistake, kissing her a disaster. He'd come too close to forgetting the past, yanking her soft body hard against his and surrendering to his raging need.

Because one thing hadn't changed. Despite the years, despite the pain, he couldn't look at that woman without wanting her. Everything about her still appealed to him. Her gentleness, her elegance, her warmth.

And leaving that bedroom had been amazingly tough to do. He'd barely slept. Instead, he'd spent hours berating himself for his weakness, fighting the urge to go back to that room and slake his lust.

He glanced at where she sat in the passenger seat, skimmed over the T-shirt that gloved her full breasts, then jerked his gaze away. But the lust wasn't the worst part of this mess. The real kicker was that he'd wanted to believe her, comfort her, *trust* her again.

The more sincere she seemed, the greater the betrayal. She'd taught him that lesson five years back.

So why was he so tempted to forget it? Why was he letting her get to him again? Trusting Sofia was idiotic, suicidal—like trying to punch a hole through a wall with his head.

Disgusted, he accelerated over the cobblestones, braked briefly at the corner, turned down Antonio's street. Damn, he didn't need this distraction.

And he didn't want her with him now. He'd intended to slip out and search Antonio's apartment while she was asleep. But his aunt had gone berserk when he'd tried to leave, claiming she'd had a premonition, convinced Sofia had been cursed for touching the necklace, insisting he get Sofia out of the apartment before her bad karma doomed them all.

He blew out another breath, squeezed the car into a parking space beside a construction Dumpster and turned the ignition off. Maybe his crazy aunt was right. Maybe he was doomed. He'd definitely lost his sanity around Sofia.

But sane or not, he was stuck with her, at least for now. And somehow he had to get them into Antonio's apartment and figure out what his partner had been up to without tipping off the police—or losing what was left of his mind.

"Okay, here's the plan," he told her. "These old buildings don't have a back entrance, so we have to go in the front. And I can't pick the lock without attracting attention."

He surveyed the narrow street. Foot traffic was light in the midday heat, but a few cars rumbled by. "I'll ring some apartments, see if someone will let us in. You watch to make sure no one's looking."

"All right." Her gaze didn't meet his, which didn't surprise him. She'd been subdued since they'd started off, skittish, as if she regretted that kiss. He wanted to forget it, too.

Too bad his body disagreed.

He waited for her to climb out of the car, locked it, then led the way down the narrow sidewalk toward Antonio's building. A motorcycle buzzed past. Dishes clattered in a nearby bar. They passed single-file below the scaffolding of a building under renovation, emerged on the other side.

But then the muscles along the back of his neck tensed. He glanced up the empty street, over to the stray pedestrians trudging along the opposite sidewalk, but they seemed more intent on talking on their cell phones and staying in the shade than noticing him and Sofia.

So why was he suddenly so jumpy?

Searching Antonio's apartment was a risk, especially with Sofia along, but he couldn't delay this trip. He needed details of Antonio's plan, clues about where the necklace might be, something that would help him fight back.

And he had to do it now, before the police searched the place or put it under surveillance.

They reached Antonio's building, and he touched her arm. "This is it." He forced his attention to the intercom beside the door, ignoring the way her breasts shifted beneath the T-shirt, the way the sunlight caressed her soft skin.

He'd rung half the apartments by the time he got lucky and someone buzzed him back. He pushed the massive door open, waited for Sofia to step over the stone threshold and followed her inside. The cool, dark air of the windowless lobby sheltered them from prying eyes.

But that edgy feeling still teased his gut, the sense that something was off. He strode through the quiet lobby, glanced at the wooden stairs spiraling around the elevator shaft, eyed the glassed-in metal cage that was creaking into view. But there was just an *anciana* in it, a tiny barrel of a woman wearing a headscarf and widow's black.

The elevator opened, and she shuffled out, pulling a small, wheeled cart behind her. Out to do her afternoon shopping. The grip on his stomach eased.

"Hola, buenas tardes," he said politely, and moved aside to let her pass. But the wheels of her pull-cart got stuck in the elevator door's groove, and she stopped. He slapped one hand over the door to keep it from closing and jerked the cart from the track.

"Gracias," the woman mumbled. She looked at him, then

at Sofia, and the muscles clenched again in his gut. But the old woman just turned away.

He followed Sofia into the elevator and let the door close. The cage lurched up, and he glanced through the glass. The woman still stood there, checking her cart. So why couldn't he shake that nagging worry that something was wrong?

"What's the matter?" Sofia asked.

He met her gaze. "I don't know." His stomach felt restless. The skin on the back of his neck tensed.

And he was losing it big time if an old lady with a shopping cart was getting to him.

He rubbed his eyes, squeezed the bridge of his nose, felt the exhaustion and tension roll through him. "It's my aunt. She's convinced we've been cursed."

"Because of the necklace? You mean because I touched it?"

"Partly." His aunt had insisted the curse was real, that any non-Roma who touched the necklace would die. "But she claims she had a premonition of danger."

Sofia blinked. "Do you believe her?"

"Sure." He lifted a brow. "You've been shot, the police are chasing us, and a killer wants us dead. So, yeah. I'd say danger's a pretty safe bet right now."

Her lips curved, and amusement lit her green eyes. "I suppose premonitions do come easy after the fact." Her smile widened, her eyes warmed even more, and she looked so soft, so alluring suddenly that it sucked the air from his lungs. And he remembered how easy it was to like her, the oasis she'd been from the world.

Dangerous thoughts, Moreno. The elevator jolted to a stop on the top floor then. Grateful, he dragged his eyes from Sofia, led the way to Antonio's door and made short work of the lock, determined to get out of there fast—before he did something really dangerous, like hauling her into his arms again.

They stepped inside to a wall of heat. The closed-up apartment sweltered in the summer sun, and sweat instantly streaked down his back. But he didn't dare turn on the air conditioner and create any noise.

"You search the kitchen and bedroom," he said, keeping his voice low. "Look for any kind of information, anything that indicates what he's been up to. I'll check the computer and desk."

"Got it." Sofia headed to the bedroom, and Luke put himself to work, checking desk drawers, scrolling through Antonio's computer files, trying to ignore the stifling heat. It was over ninety degrees in the small apartment, especially with the sunlight beating through the dormer window.

"There's nothing in the bedroom or bathroom," Sofia said a moment later. She passed by him on her way to the kitchen.

He nodded to indicate he'd heard, scanned another document, wiped the sweat dripping into his eyes. Damn, it was hot. And he couldn't find a thing on the computer. He searched the last few files, swore, flicked it off.

Sofia emerged from the kitchen then. "Nothing in there. Just this calendar by the phone."

She stopped at the desk, held out the wall calendar, flipped through the pages. "It's blank." She tossed it down, flapped her T-shirt to let in air, then blotted her face on her sleeve. "Did you find anything on the computer?"

"No, nothing." He scowled, leaned back in the desk chair, dragged his gaze from the damp fabric between her breasts. "That's the problem. It's too clean."

"What do you mean?"

"We never had a formal office. We just worked out of our apartments, met clients at the job sites. So Antonio should have notes here, plans. But there's nothing, not even a lousy backup disk."

She tilted her head. "Meaning what?"

"Meaning he either cleaned this place out or he had everything stored somewhere else."

"Like where?"

"Good question."

She chewed her lip, frowned. "How much do you know about him?"

"Not enough, obviously." He let out a bitter laugh. "I never expected a betrayal, that's for sure."

She flinched, looked away. A flush rose to her cheeks, and she crossed her arms. Oh, hell. He hadn't meant to dredge that up.

He rose, strode to the balcony window, and lifted the blinds. He heard her cross the tiled floor behind him.

"We met at the university," he said. "We were friends." Or so he'd thought. He dropped the blinds and faced her again. "We kept in touch. When my job with don Fernando fell apart, he suggested a partnership. He had the contacts. I had the expertise. It seemed like a good match. It *was* a good match, until this."

He blew out his breath. "Now I wonder if the whole thing wasn't a setup."

"You mean to get the necklace?"

"Yeah." He frowned, shook his head. "No. That doesn't make sense. No one knew that necklace existed until it showed up in the bank vault. And that was only nine months ago."

"Maybe the theft idea came later. Maybe he really was your friend, and then something happened and he changed."

"Yeah, right." He wasn't that naive.

"Luke…" She hesitated, and her gaze met his. "I meant what I said this morning. I really am sorry that I didn't believe you."

Oh, hell. He really didn't want to discuss this. Not again.

He grimaced, rubbed the back of his neck. "Let's just forget it, okay?"

"But why didn't you tell me?" she persisted. "I think, maybe if you'd said something, if I'd known—"

"That I'd been a thief? That I grew up in a slum?" He looked at her in disbelief. "What difference would that have made?"

"I don't know, but it was such a shock—"

"You wouldn't have looked at me if you'd known. You were an antiquities expert, don Fernando's protégé, part of his inner group."

"I worked there just like you did."

He scoffed. "Hardly. I didn't live at the estate."

"The room came with the job. You knew that."

"Yeah." He'd also known he had no business being around her.

His gaze roamed the elegant slant of her cheekbones, the slender line of her throat. She'd seemed like an exotic princess to him—smart, sexy, sophisticated. Totally beyond his reach. And so beautiful that he'd gone into adrenaline overload whenever she'd been around.

And the way she'd looked at him—with respect, admiration, desire. As if he hadn't grown up in the slums. As if he hadn't been rejected by his family. As if he hadn't had a criminal past. And God help him, but he would have done anything to live up to what she'd thought, to be what she'd believed him to be.

At least until she'd betrayed him.

A flat, empty feeling moved into his chest, that dead ache he'd harbored for years, and he shook his head. "It wouldn't have mattered. You would have still turned your back on me."

"That's not fair." Hurt blazed in her eyes, and she folded her arms. "You didn't give me a chance."

His gaze held hers. A sliver of doubt wormed into his mind. Maybe she was right. Maybe he hadn't given her a chance. Could she really have been as sincere as she seemed?

He closed the space between them, then stepped closer still—until he inhaled the heat of her skin, saw sweat glisten at the base of her throat, forced her to look up to meet his eyes.

"So tell me, *querida*. Would you have believed me if you'd known? Would you have risked your career for me? Taken my word over don Fernando's?"

She bit her lip. And emotions flickered through those smoky green eyes—uncertainty, doubt, guilt.

He hissed. That was his answer, right there.

"Luke," she pleaded.

"Forget it." He stepped back. "It doesn't matter." The past was gone. And he refused to let himself care.

"We need to go," he continued, disgusted that he'd nearly let her suck him in. *Again.* "We can't spend any more time here." Furious at himself, he strode back to the window and parted a slat on the blinds.

He swept his gaze up the street, yanked his mind off Sofia and his inane desire to believe her. Why did he keep letting her get to him? What was it about this woman that made him toss away common sense?

The old woman waiting at the curb with her shopping cart snagged his attention, and he focused his gaze on her. He dragged in air, let his heart rate calm, pulled his mind away from the past. But that sense of wrongness hit him again, and he scowled.

"What's wrong?" Sofia asked. She joined him at the window, peered out a slat at the street.

"I don't know." Sweat trickled down his temples. A pigeon cooed from the roof. "Something about that old woman bothers me. She should be gone by now." Even hobbling on her swollen feet, even maneuvering her cart through that construction zone, she'd had time to get to the stores.

Sofia frowned. "She might be waiting for someone to pick her up. But it's a strange time to shop with the stores still closed."

She was right. It was siesta time. The stores were closed. That construction site was silent, the workers gone.

Which meant there was only one reason that woman would be out there now. She was an informant, a spy. The cops had hired her to watch for them.

And he'd walked right into their trap.

A car pulled up in front of the woman then. Two men climbed out, spoke to her, then headed toward Antonio's building. He swore. *"La pasma."*

"The police? They're here?" Panic made her voice high.

"Yeah." He let go of the blinds and turned. "It looks like they were expecting us."

Sofia's face paled. She jerked her gaze to his. "But… How are we going to get out?"

Good question. The building had one set of stairs, one elevator. No fire escape or back door.

He narrowed his gaze on the dormer window. "I hope you don't mind heights, *querida*." And he really hoped that his aunt's premonition didn't come true. "Because the only way out is through the roof."

Chapter 7

"The roof?" Sofia blinked at him, her eyes huge. "But…you can't be serious. We're six stories up."

"It's the only way we can go." Disgusted at himself, unable to believe he'd waltzed into this trap, he strode across the room to the dormer window. It was half a meter square, barely wide enough to squeeze through. Not that they had any choice.

He unhooked the latch and shoved it open, then hoisted himself onto the sill. Hot air blasted his face. Cars clattered past on the cobblestone street six stories below.

He crawled onto the clay roof tiles barely three feet from the building's edge, then turned back to help Sofia. "Come on. Grab my hand, and I'll pull you out."

She hesitated. "But Luke, we can't—"

"We have to. Come on," he said again, as his pulse sped. "Hurry up. We need to go."

"I know, but…the roof. It's—" Sudden pounding battered the door. She jerked around, whirled back, and panic pooled in her eyes.

"Hurry." Sweat trickled down his neck. His thighs ached from balancing on the slanted roof. Damn, they needed to go.

But she just stood there, blinking, wobbling. And his hopes tanked. If he couldn't get her onto the roof…

But then she inhaled sharply. Her eyes locked on his. And she reached up and grabbed his hand.

Trusting him.

A sudden warmth unfurled in his chest.

His palms sweating now, he tugged her through the opening to the roof. She crawled out, glanced down at the street and gasped.

"Don't look down." He kept one hand firmly on her trembling arm and closed the window behind them. It wasn't much of a decoy but might buy them a minute or two.

"I've got you. Come on." He helped her rise, led her away from the edge to the apex of the roof, then surveyed the sea of orange tiles. The buildings along this side of the street were all connected, sprawling before them like erratic steps. "We need to find a terrace or another window we can climb back through."

Sofia wheezed in answer, and he glanced back. "Are you okay?"

"I'm…fine."

Hardly. Her eyes had that dazed, frozen-in-the-headlights look, and she had a death grip on the back of his shirt. But no matter how rattled she was, they had to hurry. The cops could storm out here at any time.

He blinked away the sweat blurring his eyes, then towed her toward the building beside them. The August sun blazed down. Pigeons fluttered and cooed nearby. The round tiles baked in the brutal heat and sizzled the soles of his shoes.

And there wasn't another window in sight.

At the edge of the building, he stopped, eyed the one-story drop to the adjoining roof. "I'll go first." He glanced back. "But you need to let go of my shirt, *querida*."

"Oh, right." She dropped the shirt, managed a shaky smile, and his admiration sparked. He knew she was scared, but she hadn't complained or balked.

He leaped down easily, then turned back and reached for her. She scooted over the side, and he caught her, his hands on her slender waist. She clung to him, and he held her for a moment, giving her time to regain her balance, conscious of her curving waist, the long legs shaking against his.

And despite the urgency, he was tempted to pull her closer yet.

"You're doing great," he said, and dropped his hands. Better than he'd expected with her injured leg.

She shot him another strained smile, latched onto his T-shirt again, and they crept across the next roof. He squinted through the shimmering sunlight, scanned the rooftops, finally spotted a dormer window off to the side.

"There's a window," he said and nodded toward it. "That will take us back inside."

But then the pigeons near them squawked and flapped into the air, enveloping them in a riot of beating wings. He glanced back, saw a flash of blue on Antonio's roof, and his heart stopped.

A cop. They'd just run out of time.

"Down here," he whispered, his pulse thudding fast now. He jumped to the next roof. She slipped down beside him, and he urged her against the wall. They huddled together, motionless, waiting to find out if that cop had seen them.

Seconds ticked by. The sun blazed down. Sweat trickled down his jaw and pasted his shirt to his back. He glanced at

Sofia, struck by how calm she'd stayed, how quickly she'd reacted despite her fear.

Minutes later, the pigeons settled around them again, cooed, and pecked the tiles. He rose, peeked over the edge of the wall, and released his breath.

"Is he gone?" Sofia whispered.

"I think so. But he could be waiting, calling for backup."

"So we'd better not head for that window."

"No. We'd be too exposed." But continuing the way they were going—across the building under renovation—would be tough. Bare patches and broken tiles littered the sagging roof.

"You think we can walk on that?" Sofia asked, echoing his doubts.

"We'll find out." He tugged her to her feet, met her gaze, and a sudden fear for her scraped through his gut. "Just watch your step." He didn't need her to fall through the roof.

He started across, picking his way carefully through the shattered tiles, trying to avoid the most treacherous spots. But the old clay was brittle. It cracked under his weight, sending loose pieces tumbling toward the edge.

"Luke, look," Sofia said from behind him, and he whipped back. "Over there. Is that a terrace?"

He glanced at the next building over, exhaled in relief. "Yeah. That's perfect." Forty feet to go and they had a way back down to the street.

He started toward it, hurrying now, but another tile shifted under his foot. He staggered, reached back to steady Sofia, lost his balance and fell. His shoulder hit the roof, and he slid.

"Luke!" Sofia lunged toward him, still clutching his shirt. His momentum pulled her down with him. She slid forward, shrieked.

"Let go!" He grabbed the tiles, grappled for a handhold, but they broke loose, and he skidded more. "Let go!" he shouted again, but she hung on.

His T-shirt stretched, stretched even more. She clenched the shirt, sobbed his name. His fear for her pulsed in his throat. He was moving too fast. He'd pull her down with him. "Sofia—"

She slid toward him, lost her grip, and Luke skidded toward the edge, bumping over tiles, picking up speed. His feet plunged into the air. He made a desperate grab for a handhold, caught the jagged edge of a tile. It knifed into his fingers but he clutched it, holding on, holding on.

His breath rasped and heaved. Sweat poured into his eyes. A motorcycle zipped past on the street below. He heard Sofia's ragged sobs.

But he'd stopped. He was still on the roof. He cautiously lifted one foot, searched carefully for a toehold. One wrong move, and he'd plummet to the sidewalk below.

He wedged his foot between the tiles, then pushed, inching himself up, away from the edge. His fingers trembled and throbbed. His biceps and shoulders ached.

He eased his face past the broken tile, shifted his hands, his feet, crawled farther away from the edge. Then he closed his eyes and gasped for breath. The sun sizzled his neck, his back. Adrenaline charged through his limbs.

Damn, that was close. He'd nearly fallen. Died.

And so had Sofia.

Fear slashed into anger, and he jerked up his head. "Damn it, why didn't you let go? Do you have any idea how dangerous that was? You could have been killed!"

But she didn't answer. She just huddled on the roof, shaking, rocking back and forth.

He blew out his breath. Oh, hell, it wasn't her fault.

She'd just saved his miserable life. If she hadn't held on, if she hadn't broken his fall, he'd be splattered on the sidewalk right now.

He climbed back to where she sat and perched beside her. He hung his head, hauled in air, felt the strong, rough beat of his pulse. Sweat streamed down his jaw, his neck.

But he had to get a grip, get them off the roof, no matter how shaken up they were. Every cop in Madrid must have heard that noise.

But Sofia was trembling, gasping in air, clearly near her limit. "Come on." He gentled his voice. "Let's go."

He pushed himself to his feet, held out his good hand. Still shuddering, she peeled her fingers from the tiles, grabbed his hand and rose.

He led her the last few feet to the narrow terrace, and jumped down. He helped her to solid ground, then pulled her to the wall, away from the sliding glass doors.

"Luke," she whispered. "You almost…you almost…"

"Shh." Sensing she needed a second to rest, to come down from the shock, he enveloped her in his arms. Then he stroked her back, her neck, absorbing her shudders, her fear. She pressed her cheek to his chest, quivered against him, and his own fear churned through his gut.

Because in that instant back there when he'd nearly lost her…

He closed his eyes, pulled in his breath, willing away the horror, the fear. He exhaled, letting his heartbeat steady and slow. Sofia finally relaxed against him and sighed.

Then she raised her head, and her gaze met his. And he looked at her, just looked at her for a moment, at her beautiful gray-green eyes, her face. Her face was close, so close, her lips just inches from his, soft, curving, *alive.* Her breasts brushed his chest, soft and full; her hip curved into his thigh.

He slid his hand up her back, around the dip of her waist. She felt warm, soft, lush.

And suddenly, he wanted to touch her skin, stroke her breasts, make the tips pebble hard in his palms.

Her breath hitched. Her smoky eyes darkened on his. And he flashed back to that morning in the bedroom—the way she'd moved, the way she'd smelled, the way she'd kissed.

"Luke," she whispered. She raised her hand to his jaw.

The soft touch whipped through him like lightning. And just once, he didn't want to fight the need anymore. Just this once, he didn't want to think about the past.

He pulled her close, dipped his head, fit her feminine body to his. Then he slanted his mouth over hers, surrendering to the hunger, the heat. She was lush, moist, hot. Everything he'd ever wanted, what he'd desired.

His heart kicked, drummed hard, and he deepened the kiss, going harder, longer, losing himself in her mouth, in her heat. And he wanted to taste her skin, lick her sweat, make her shudder and gasp. Take her every way he could.

And she melted against him, pressing herself to him, making that soft, sweet moan that welcomed him home.

Home? He stilled. What was he thinking? This woman wasn't a refuge for him. Not anymore. He couldn't trust her. Plus, they were still on the roof, exposed. The police could be here at any time.

He wrenched his mouth away, beat back the need, battled his way from the heat. His heart thundered in protest. His lungs labored to draw in air. And she blinked up at him, her hair wild, her eyes unfocused, and he wanted to grab her and kiss her again.

He tipped his head back against the wall and closed his eyes. He couldn't deal with this now. They had to keep moving, get to a safer place.

"Stay here." His voice croaked out, rusty, raw. He tore himself from her side, shocked at the effort that took.

Then, still fighting the lust, he crept to the sliding glass door. A woman sat inside on the sofa, eating, the television blaring. He jerked back, his heart thumping again, and switched to the other glass door. An empty bedroom. He motioned for Sofia to follow, slid the glass open, and they sneaked inside.

The bedroom was small and hot, the hallway deserted. He inched to the front door with Sofia behind him, undid the lock and chain. Then he opened the door, and they slipped outside.

He didn't pause. He grabbed her hand, pulled her down the creaking stairs. Three flights later, they reached the lobby door.

He tugged it open, peeked out, swept his gaze up the street, then back toward Antonio's apartment. A group of students was heading toward them, laughing, clowning around, followed by half a dozen uniformed cops.

He swore. The cops must have heard those tiles fall, figured out where they were. And they'd wasted valuable time indulging in that kiss.

He shut the door, thought hard. There wasn't another exit. They had to go out this way.

"We'd better split up," he decided. "You go out first. There's a kiosk just up the street. Buy a magazine, then wait by the curb. Act casual and try not to limp." He paused. "Do you have any money?"

She shook her head. "I lost my purse at the palace."

He dug in his pocket, handed her a ten-euro bill. "Here. But whatever you do, don't talk. Your accent will give you away."

"All right."

"I'll get the car and come back. Watch for me."

Cursing himself again for letting that kiss distract him, he cracked the heavy door open and watched. The students came closer, closer. "Okay, go," he urged. She stepped out and started toward the kiosk.

He waited a few more seconds, his nerves winding tighter, higher, then slipped in with the noisy teens. He strolled along with them, dodging the motorcycles parked on the narrow sidewalk, the low, metal posts lining the curb.

They walked past the kiosk—Sofia browsed through the magazines, good, good—then up the sidewalk toward the car. A police car sped down the road, then another, and the muscles of his shoulders tensed. But he resisted the urge to look back.

When they reached his aunt's car, he veered off from the group and climbed inside. He closed the door, his heart jack-hammering against his rib cage, and finally glanced down the street. Several cops charged into the building they'd just vacated. Another planted himself against the wall outside the door, his eyes on Sofia. Was he suspicious or just admiring her curves?

Regardless, Luke had to hurry. He started the car, cruised down the one-way street, then raced around the block. He pulled up to the kiosk just as the cop pushed away from the wall.

Come on, Luke urged as the cop headed toward her. He was only a dozen feet away.

The cop called something out, but Sofia ignored him. She limped to the car, jumped in and shut the door. The cop ran up, his weapon drawn. Luke slammed the accelerator down and sped off.

He raced toward the corner, the car's tires racketing over the cobblestones, and glanced in his rearview mirror. The cop ran into the street, his weapon raised. Luke swore, swerved, careered around the corner, then zigzagged through the streets of Madrid.

When they reached Calle de Atocha, he finally exhaled. He merged into the heavy traffic, confident their small white Ford would blend in.

For now. But he knew the reprieve wouldn't last.

He scowled, accelerated past a slow-moving truck, disgusted at the mess he'd made. No doubt that cop had caught their tag number, or part of it, at least. Now the police would run it through their computers and make the connection to his aunt—which meant they had a few hours, a day at most, to get out of Madrid.

"Luke, your hand," Sofia said.

He flicked his gaze to his fingers where the tiles had sliced him, ignored the blood, the throb. "I'll live."

"But we need to stop the bleeding." She rummaged in the glove compartment, pulled out a rag. "Hold out your hand and I'll wrap it."

"Forget it." He didn't need her soft hands anywhere near him after that kiss. "Just give it to me."

He grabbed the rag, wadded it against the steering wheel, and returned his gaze to the road, determined to block out memories of that kiss. Because he knew one thing. This woman was dangerous. Those velvet curves, those sultry eyes got to him every time.

And if he wasn't careful, she'd have him letting down his guard and believing her again.

So he forced himself to focus on maneuvering through the erratic traffic, figuring out where they could get another car, where they could hide. But he was no closer to finding a solution by the time they reached his aunt's apartment.

Even worse, as he rode up the elevator with Sofia, a sense of impending danger crept through his gut. He didn't believe in premonitions, but a deep anxiety, the urge to hurry, hurry, began beating through his brain.

"Luke," Sofia whispered, and he slid his gaze to her. Her face had turned pale, her knuckles white on the elevator rail. "Do you feel...danger?"

"Yeah." He couldn't deny it.

And as soon as they reached his aunt's floor, that sense of wrongness spun through him again, making his gut tighten even more.

He stepped out of the elevator, saw that her door was ajar, and his stomach plunged. If anything had happened to his aunt...

He grabbed Sofia's arm and pulled her away from the open doorway. "Stay out here," he told her, his voice low. "And if I don't come out in a few minutes, leave."

"What? I'm not going to leave you!"

"You have to. I mean it." He gave her a shake, needing her to listen, to obey. He couldn't put her in danger again. "If I don't come back, you need to go." He pulled the car keys from his pocket and pressed them into her hand.

"But Luke, I can't—"

"Damn it. You have to go." The urgency washed through him again, pushed into his throat. "Promise me."

"But—"

"For God's sake, Sofia. Please." She frowned, opened her mouth as if she wanted to argue, but closed it and took the keys.

Hoping she obeyed him, he turned and sneaked into the apartment. He listened now, his vision tunneling, every sense still and alert. An unnatural silence pulsed in the air, a feeling of danger. A shiver skimmed down his back, bristled his hair.

Then a rustling sound came from the kitchen, and he froze. He waited, his blood thudding in his ears.

And then a woman moaned.

His heart stopped, raced. He peeked around the corner, spotted his aunt on the floor, blood pooling beneath her chest.

He rushed to her, dropped to one knee, inhaled the harsh stench of blood. *"Tía. Tía Carmen, háblame."*

"Lucas?" Her eyes fluttered open, closed. Blood. There was so much blood. It soaked her blouse, oozed onto the floor. And she was pale, too pale. He grabbed her wrist, searched for a pulse, while his own heart reeled in his throat.

His fault. This was his fault. He never should have come here. He'd brought the danger here, left her alone, ignored her warning, her fears.

He felt the air move behind him, whirled, as Sofia rushed over and knelt beside them.

"Oh, God." Her face was white, her eyes huge, stricken. "Is she—"

"I don't know." He leaned closer, held his hand to his aunt's mouth. Seconds passed. Fear streaked up his spine, clamped down his lungs.

Then his aunt's faint breath brushed his palm. "She's alive." Barely. But they needed to get her help fast.

Sofia leaped up and grabbed a dishtowel, while he rose and strode to the phone. He called an ambulance first, then his cousin Manolo, who lived downstairs.

He tossed the phone aside and returned to his aunt. Sofia held the woman's hand, stroked her forehead, made soft, soothing noises, pressed the towel against her chest.

"Lucas," his aunt whispered, and he crouched closer to hear. *"Vete. Hay...peligro. Mucho."*

Danger. "Who was it?" he asked in Spanish. "The cops?"

"No...luna...dengues malos." The moon. Bad spirits? She was delirious, out of her head.

She groaned, thrashed. More blood seeped from her chest.

"Stay still. Don't move." He glanced blindly around. Where was that ambulance? If it didn't get here soon, she'd bleed to death.

His aunt clutched his wrist. Her fingers were frail, cold, like frigid cobwebs tickling his skin. *"Vete."* Go.

"Don't talk," he pleaded. "Just hang on. The ambulance is on the way."

But she was right. They had to leave. He glanced at Sofia, kept his voice low. "When my cousin gets here, we need to go."

"What?" She sounded shocked. "We can't leave your aunt."

"We have to. The police will be here. And she's safer if we're not around."

"But—"

"Sofia, think about it. This guy shot Antonio in the head. One shot, point-blank. So why didn't he do that here? Why shoot her in the gut?" *Why make an innocent old woman suffer?*

Sofia looked at his aunt, at him, her eyes bleak. "I don't know."

"He wanted to torture her." *Torture him.* He was like a cat toying with a mouse before the kill.

"It's a message. A warning." That he knew him. That he could find him—anywhere, anytime. That no one connected to him was safe.

His eyes shot to Sofia. Fear slithered down his spine, raw dread that strangled his breath.

Because he knew what the real message was—that unless he stopped him, Sofia would be next.

Chapter 8

It was her fault. Luke's aunt had been attacked because of her.

Sofia rubbed the ache mauling her forehead, tried to beat back the horror, the guilt, but the truth kept echoing through her brain. They'd stayed with Luke's aunt because of Sofia's gunshot wound. And now his aunt had been shot, might not survive—because of her.

The car hit a rut, jolted out, and she grabbed the door and held on. They'd taken a convoluted route through the mountains west of Madrid to this abandoned pasture, searching for a safe place to rest. But how could they outrun a vicious killer? How could they possibly hide?

Hysteria mushroomed inside her. That killer was out there—watching them, tracking them, hunting them down.... Her gaze darted from the low-growing shrubs to a thick stand of pines, and she sucked in a long, reedy breath. He couldn't be here. Not yet. She had to tamp back the fear and calm down.

Luke stopped by a crumbling stone hut and cut the engine. Silence engulfed the car. Birds chirped in the cooling air. It was ten o'clock, peaceful as the sun finally slid behind the parched hills.

But there was nothing peaceful about her life anymore. It had careered completely beyond her control.

"We'll rest here for a few hours," Luke announced.

He climbed out, then crunched through the dried grass to the hut. He'd been silent since they'd left Madrid, brooding, his dark face set in angry lines. Angry at her, no doubt. After that brutal attack on his aunt, he probably didn't want her around.

Guilt squeezed her chest. She didn't blame him for being furious. And she owed him another apology, fast. Not that it would do any good—there were no magic words that could help his aunt. But at least she had to try.

Ignoring the fierce ache searing her leg, she got out, grabbed the food and bottled water Luke had bought as they'd left Madrid and followed him inside. The hut was musty, dark. She set the groceries on the wooden table, making it totter on the uneven floor. Luke tugged a bottle of water from the six-pack and prowled back out.

She eyed the narrow bed lining one wall, paused. God, she was tired. She was filthy, starving, her body so battered that she wanted to cry. But she couldn't rest yet. She had to help make plans, figure out what to do—and apologize to Luke for his aunt.

She found him leaning against the hood of the car. He tipped his head back as she approached, took a swallow of water, then stared toward a cluster of trees. She let her gaze trace the line of his throat, the wide shoulders slumped with fatigue. And a longing welled inside her, a need to stroke him, hold him, soothe his exhaustion, his pain.

Instead, she stood beside him, turned to watch a hawk ride the thermals in search of prey, tried to figure out what to say. "Luke."

Her throat tightened. She swallowed, tried again. "I'm sorry about your aunt. I know we went there because of me, because of my leg, and I…I'm so sorry. I never dreamed that she'd be hurt."

"It's not your fault." He sounded disgusted, tired. "I should have known better. And I never should have left her alone."

"Can you find out how she is?"

"Yeah, I'll call my cousin from a pay phone when we get to a town."

She nodded, rubbed her arms, inhaled the peaceful scent of grass. But anxiety still drummed at the base of her skull, the worry that the killer was out there, watching—and that she was somehow to blame.

Luke gulped down the last of his water, frowned, wiped his mouth on the back of his hand. "What I don't get is how they found us so fast. No one knows I used to live there."

Her heart skipped. She'd told don Fernando, of course. But he wouldn't have told anyone. Unless…

Her stomach plunged. She raised her hand to her throat. What if she had tipped that killer off?

She made a small, thin sound of distress, and Luke shot her a glance. His eyes narrowed on hers, darkened, and then he went totally still.

Her cheeks burned. Her heart beat fast. She knew her guilt was all over her face. "I phoned don Fernando this morning," she admitted.

Luke didn't move. His face remained frozen, his jaw rigid beneath the black stubble. Only his eyes flickered with emotions—shock, disbelief, disgust.

"I needed to warn him about Paco," she said in a rush. "He

asked me where I was. He was so worried, really scared for me, so I told him. I wanted him to know I was all right."

A dull flush crept up Luke's cheeks. The muscle in his hard jaw flexed. He looked furious, the angriest she'd ever seen him.

Her stomach plunged. "Luke, I'm sorry. I never thought…"

He looked away, his jaw working with a vengeance. Tension vibrated from his muscled frame.

Then his gaze slammed back into hers, and she took an instinctive step back. "Do you think this is a game?" he said. "Don't you understand that they're trying to kill us?"

"But don Fernando would never hurt us." Misery chugged through her gut. "I know he wouldn't. Paco must have found out somehow."

He hissed at that, his disgust obvious. "You can't be that naive."

She crossed her arms. Was Luke right? *Was* she being naive? Did this prove he had tipped Paco off? It certainly looked that way.

"But why would he be involved in this?" she asked. "It doesn't make any sense. He doesn't need the money. He protects antiquities. He donates money for restorations, the *patrimonio cultural.*

"And even if he were involved—which I still don't believe—he never would have hurt your aunt. He's one of the gentlest people I know."

"Very touching." His gaze raked her, and his eyes turned stonier yet. "So tell me, *querida.* Just how does he get loyalty like that? What the hell does he do for you?"

She gasped. "What?" He made her relationship with don Fernando sound sordid, as if he'd bought her off—or worse. "It's not what you think. He's not—"

But Luke shoved away from the car. He stalked to the edge

of the hut, then stood there, his back stiff, fury pouring from his rigid frame.

She hugged her arms, feeling sick. He didn't understand. And he didn't know her at all. But how could he? She never talked about her past. Never. No one knew, not even don Fernando.

Her stomach fluttered, dipped like the swallows swooping around the hut. Maybe she owed him the truth. She'd hurt him deeply—now and in the past. Not intentionally, but by staying silent, by trying to protect herself, she had ended up wounding him. So maybe it was time she explained.

Not sure where to begin, she limped over to where he stood. She rubbed her arms, summoned her strength, prayed that he'd give her a chance.

"Luke… I'd like to explain why I owe him so much."

"Forget it." He folded his arms, scowled toward the trees, and a bleak feeling seeped through her gut.

"Please." He had to listen. "It's just that…" *The rocks.* It always boiled down to the rocks. She straightened her shoulders and tried again.

"You see… There was this rock pile by my house when I was a kid. It was nothing really, just a bunch of rocks somebody dumped off there, but there were these ones that sparkled—mica, but I didn't know that then. I thought they were beautiful, magical. I used to sit there for hours and grind away at the rocks, making fairy dust."

He looked at her as if she were demented. "So?"

"So I spent a lot of time out there alone. I was sick a lot with ear infections, bronchitis and I missed a lot, of school, and my mom…" She shifted her gaze to the hills, rubbed her arms. "I guess she didn't like having a sick kid around. It was too much work, she said, with her being single and all. So one day, when I was six, she just…didn't come home."

She closed her eyes, struggled to breathe. To fight through the misery, admit the terrible shame in words. "I thought the magic would bring her back, make her…love me again. So I sat out there for days, just grinding away at those rocks, sprinkling the dust around."

She pressed her hands to her lips and blinked hard. Trying to hold back the hurt, push down the pain. But the raw, harsh truth churned through her gut. She hadn't been worth her mother's love.

"Dumb, huh?" She shook her head, shot him a wobbly smile. "A neighbor finally noticed that she wasn't around and called the police. And I got sent to my first foster home.

"I think I missed that rock pile more than my mom." Or maybe thinking about her mother just hurt too much, as well as the father she'd never known.

"Anyway, I didn't do much better in the foster homes. I was shy, gawky, sick." A constant bother, one foster father had told her. Not worth the friggin' paycheck. "So I didn't stay in one place long."

She braved a glance at Luke. He still scowled into the distance, but at least he hadn't moved away. "Then one day, in the seventh grade, we went to a museum on a field trip, and I saw a collection of Baltic amber. It was the most beautiful thing I'd ever seen."

She smiled, remembering her amazement, her awe, the absolute wonder of those gems. "It was like finding the rock pile again, only better. I was so caught up in the collection that I missed the bus back to school.

"I didn't even care about the punishment. I was hooked. I started reading everything I could about amber. I studied, worked odd jobs, saved my money so I could start my own collection. And when I was sixteen, I finally bought my very first piece of amber—except it turned out to be copal, a fake."

She slanted Luke a glance. "I should have known better, but... I was devastated. All that money I'd saved... But it taught me a lesson." That you couldn't change what something was. That you could disguise it, pretend it was something else for a while, but the truth would always show through.

"I didn't want to be fooled again, so I studied harder. I learned how to run tests, how to authenticate a piece, how to produce a fake.

"I started making reproductions during college. I worked for some jewelers, had an internship at a local museum. That's how I caught the attention of don Fernando. He got me the fellowship in Kaliningrad, studying with the master carvers."

She looked at Luke's rigid profile, willing him to understand. "Don Fernando changed my life. He opened up a whole new world for me. For the first time, people paid attention to me. They wanted me, accepted me. I made reproductions for celebrities, museums, insurance companies. I did appraisals, got called to consult.

"Then he offered me the job here, cataloging his collection. He let me into his circle, opened his home." The only home she'd had since she was a kid. "That's when I met you."

She paused, let her gaze roam those beautifully sculpted shoulders and corded arms, the dark stubble that coated his throat. He'd been the sexiest man she'd ever seen—still was. And everything about him had intrigued her, from his amazing mind and magic hands to that outrageously handsome face.

"I couldn't believe you were interested in me. I thought...I was living a fairy tale, that I'd turned into a princess. Living in a palace, working with gems." Making love to the most incredible man on earth.

And she'd been so scared that he would see through her veneer, that he'd realize that the elegance was a sham.

But just like with that piece of copal, the shell had finally shattered, and the truth had come out. "They said you'd never cared about me, that you had lots of other women, that you…you'd just used me to get to the gems."

Luke swiveled his head, and his whiskey-colored eyes skewered hers. "And you believed them. You really thought I'd do that."

Her lips trembled. She pressed them together hard and blinked back tears. They both knew it was true.

"I thought… I didn't think…" She dragged in her breath and laid herself bare. "There wasn't any other reason you'd want me."

For a moment, he didn't move. He just stared at her, his eyes filled with incredulity, disgust. And then he turned and strode away.

She drew in a shaky breath, trying to breathe past the terrible ache crushing her chest, the void that hollowed her gut. And she stood there, alone in the rocky field, watching him walk away. He was so strong, so independent. The only man she'd ever wanted, ever loved.

A huge wave of despair flooded through her, and she hugged herself hard to stem the pain. Don Fernando had offered her the world, the acceptance she'd always craved. But Luke… Luke had offered her heaven.

But she hadn't had the guts to believe him.

Luke strode through the rock-strewn field, seething over Sofia's betrayal. She'd called don Fernando. She'd tipped the killer off. She'd trusted her patron instead of him. *Again.*

He paused at the stand of oak trees, spotted a pond down the slope and headed toward it, his anger mounting with every step. Why hadn't she believed him? She'd seen the killer shoot Antonio. She'd known he was on their trail. How much proof did she need?

He reached the rock-lined *estanque,* stripped off his clothes and plunged in. The water was deep, cold, and he dove under, welcoming the bracing lash to his skin. Then he swam back and forth, fast, furious, lap after lap, venting his frustration, his rage. Pushing himself, punishing himself until his shoulders tired, slowed by fatigue from the past two days.

And as exhaustion set in, draining the anger away, he realized that it was no use. He touched bottom, shook the water from his face, rubbed eyes gritty from lack of sleep.

And he had to admit that he believed her. No matter how offended he wanted to feel, no matter how much her betrayal stung, no matter how much he wanted to hold on to the rage, he knew that she'd told him the truth.

Oh, hell. He waded out of the pond, used his T-shirt to dry the water from his skin, tugged his jeans and shoes back on. He didn't want to sympathize with her. He especially didn't want to trust her. He refused to be that vulnerable to anyone again.

But he could picture her on that rock pile—a lost, lonely kid trying to find magic in some glittery stones.

Because he'd been just as lonely, just as lost. But he'd found his salvation in locks.

He slung his shirt over his shoulder, climbed the slope to the trees. So she wasn't the privileged princess he'd thought. She'd scrabbled her way to the top just as he had, a difficult thing to do. Maybe don Fernando had helped her, but it was her talent and tenacity that had pulled her through. And he respected her, admired her for that.

And he knew just how much that hard-won acceptance meant.

And he had to acknowledge something else—that the same gentle, trusting part of her nature that had been an oasis for him made her a target for don Fernando. That vulture had played her perfectly, hit her where she was most insecure.

The question was *why*.

He reached the trees, saw Sofia limping toward him, and stopped. Her face was flushed, her short hair wild. She looked battered and exhausted, and his sympathy rose even more. "There's a pond down there if you want to rinse off," he said.

Her gaze flicked to his bare chest, veered away. "That sounds good."

He watched her for a moment, and her gaze returned to his. The evening shadows softened her cheeks, darkened her eyes. And he realized again just how beautiful she was.

She managed an awkward smile, a tiny shrug, then headed down the hill. He turned and watched the swing of her hips, the sway of her perfect butt.

She'd thought he hadn't desired her. He closed his eyes and groaned. She had no idea just how badly he'd ached for her back then, how he'd done everything he could to be around her. He'd sat in her workshop for hours, just watching her, hypnotized by how she'd roll the gems in her hands, sniff them, caress them. Her breath would speed up, her body tense as she disappeared into her own special world, entranced, almost aroused, as if the gems were her lovers, alive. And he'd just stared at her, mesmerized by her face, watching her lips move while she explained how she loved their feel, their scent.

He'd felt the same way about her.

Hell, she'd had him so hot he couldn't breathe straight.

He opened his eyes, dragged in a breath, watched her pause at the edge of the pond. She slipped off her shoes, peeled the jeans down her thighs, exposing her long, smooth legs to his gaze.

He should walk away, give her privacy—he knew that. But he stood there, rooted, unable to move. She hesitated, glanced around, then stripped off her T-shirt and bra.

His heart stopped. Blood plunged from his head to his groin. Her breasts were full, pale, lush. And so perfect he couldn't breathe.

She waded into the water, and he tracked each step, riveted by the provocative way her breasts swayed, the tempting dip of her back. His breath grew shallow, fast, his body rock hard inside his jeans.

He flexed his fingers, the warm, soft feel of her imprinted on his cells. And he remembered the way she'd moved, the way she'd moaned, the way she'd gasped.

She bent, splashed water on her face, her arms. And he had to face another harsh truth. He wanted her. Damn, how he wanted her—under him, over him, again and again, until they were both so sated that their brains fried.

But he knew that it wasn't enough. He wanted more than a night of hot sex. He wanted her approval, her respect. Her trust.

God help him, but he wanted to redeem himself in her eyes.

Which meant he had to expose don Fernando. He had to prove to her that her patron had planned that heist.

He dragged his hand down his bristly face, tried to think through the thick haze of lust. They both needed to rest or they'd collapse. They needed to sleep for a few hours, eat.

But then they would take the offensive, do something no one would expect. They'd drive to Ávila and break into her patron's estate.

And recover the Roma necklace.

His gaze lingered on Sofia's skin, the soft curves shrouded by the gathering dusk. And he knew that he couldn't fight this lust anymore. He didn't want this attraction, didn't understand it, but he sure as hell couldn't ignore it. She was an ache in his blood, a craving that kept crashing back.

And soon, he was going to make love to Sofia again.

Chapter 9

Something had changed between them. Flutters rose in Sofia's belly as Luke parked on one of the narrow side streets in Ávila, just below the medieval wall. He glanced at her again, and even in the dark, she could see the banked heat simmering in his eyes, the way his gaze caressed her mouth. Her cheeks warmed, and she jerked her eyes away. Ever since she'd bared her soul, he'd been pinning her with hot, scorching glances that made her skin burn and stomach jump.

Of course, it didn't help that they were about to commit another crime.

She pulled in her breath, pressed her hand against her belly to quiet her nerves. It was four in the morning, dark and still, the streets mostly deserted since the bars had closed. She studied the ancient wall looming above them, stark and forbidding in the spotlights, looking as impenetrable now as it had been a thousand years ago.

"Are you sure we need to do this?" she asked.

"It's the only way to get proof."

"*If* he did it." Her gaze met his again.

"He did."

She heard the steel in his voice. He was convinced of don Fernando's guilt, that the necklace would be in his palace. She disagreed, but maybe now they could put that to rest.

"We can't run forever," he added.

"I know." Between the killer and the police, someone would eventually catch them. And if they hoped to protect themselves, they needed information, a way to locate that necklace fast. She nibbled her lip, glanced at the massive wall. "But breaking in to the palace seems awfully extreme." Not to mention dangerous.

"We'll be fine."

"As long as the security system hasn't changed."

"Yeah."

That was the big unknown, the question Luke had been grilling her on since they'd left the shepherd's hut. He had created the system, even built himself a secret backdoor to get inside, and she knew the access codes and palace routine from living at the estate. But what if something had been altered during the past five years, something neither would know?

Luke climbed out of the car, and she followed, her nerves ratcheted tight in the quiet night. Their car doors thudding shut sounded like cell doors slamming behind them.

They were committed now.

Luke fiddled with his watch. "Twenty-eight minutes. Let's go."

Her anxiety rising, she hurried up the hill with him toward the ancient wall that ringed the medieval city. He had outlined his plan on the drive over. Even with the access codes, they couldn't get through the front door of the palace without tripping over the guards. Instead, they would enter the compound via the wall.

She glanced up at the ancient battlement where sentries had once patrolled. During the day, the historic wall was open to the public. Visitors paid a fee, then strolled along the restored sections, enjoying the view.

But the wall wasn't open now. So they had to break in, hike the wall to the treacherous, unrepaired section that backed don Fernando's palace, then enter his garden through the ancient steps.

And hope they didn't trigger an unknown alarm in the meantime.

They passed one of the towers built into the wall, their footsteps echoing ominously on the cobblestone road, then entered the *puerta,* a huge, arched entrance that tunneled through the massive stone. Halfway through the arch, they stopped at a wooden door, the entrance to the walkway above. But just as Luke began to examine the lock, a group of teens strolled toward them, singing, laughing, heading home after a summer night out.

Sofia's heart tripped, beat fast. What if those kids recognized them? Their photos were all over the news. "Luke," she whispered.

"Yeah." He stepped close, then crowded her against the door. He planted one hand on the wall behind her, the other on her waist. His rough voice rumbled in her ear. "Put your arms around me."

"Right." She slid her hands up his rock-hard biceps, around his powerful shoulders and back. The voices grew louder, closer, but then he dipped his head, and she was distracted by his breath fanning her ear, the warm male scent of his skin.

His whiskered jaw brushed her cheek, and the erotic feel of it sent pleasure rippling over her skin. His lips grazed her jaw, and her pulse tapped a frenzied beat. She knew they were pretending to be lovers on their way home after a date. But if she just turned her head…

His lips skimmed her throat, and her heart sped up. His hand crept to her ribs, paused close to her breast, and suddenly, she couldn't breathe. Then his thumb stroked up. Desire sizzled through her, and she gasped.

He lifted his head. His eyes burned into hers—dark, hungry, hot. Her blood rioted in her veins.

"Damn," he whispered.

Then his lips covered hers in a hot, deep kiss that blasted away her thoughts. She clung to him, clutching his shoulders, kissing him back, absorbing his heat, his power, lost in the wonder of Luke. Desire shocked through her nerves, raced up and down her body like a delirious current, jolting her again and again. His hands roamed her back, her bottom. Then he cupped her, pulling her tightly against him. The hard feel of him scalded her blood.

She shuddered, sagged, desperate to get closer yet, but he pulled back and inched up his head. Still holding her, he glanced around, while she struggled to breathe, to think. She was panting, her heart sprinting. And then she remembered where they were, what they were doing, that the group of teens was long gone.

And that this was only an act.

Except that Luke was rigid against her. His rough breath sawed in her ear. Need hitched into her throat, and she moaned.

His eyes met hers again, burned. For an eternity he didn't move. "Later," he finally rasped. He let her go and stepped back.

Later. Dizzy, she braced her hand against the wall while Luke went to work on the lock. She inhaled, exhaled, tried to focus on their surroundings, battling the urge to launch herself against him, drag him to the ground. How could one kiss, one whispered word shatter her senses like that?

Maybe it was the adrenaline, the danger. Or maybe it was the man. Five years ago, her reaction to Luke had been the same—instant, primal, raw.

The door to the tower creaked open, and Luke motioned her inside. He closed it behind them, plunging them into musty darkness, and she grabbed the handrail attached to the wall. She hobbled after him up the winding stone steps to the gallery door.

And with every step, that one graveled word, *later,* kept thundering through her head. And so did the memories of Luke—the sexy way he'd focused on her, the intensity in those golden eyes… He'd been an amazing lover, demanding, taking her higher and harder each time. Arousing her, tormenting her…

She shivered, followed him out the tower door onto the wall walk. He'd been perfect, all right—and that was the problem. How could she possibly make love to him again and protect her heart?

He paused, and the haze from the spotlights below, the almost-full moon overhead shadowed the angles of his face. He glanced at her, stilled, and she clutched her hands, knowing he could see the need in her eyes, the desire.

Later, he'd said. And he was right. She closed her eyes, inhaled, fought for control. She couldn't think about Luke now. She needed to concentrate on getting them into the palace, keeping them safe.

She opened her eyes, forced her gaze from Luke to the path ahead. The wall was crenellated on the outside edge, resembling a long line of giant stone teeth, and high enough to shield them from view. But on the other side, there was only a handrail, making them visible to anyone in the city who glanced up.

Luke examined his watch. "Nineteen minutes. Let's move."

He strode off, and she limped behind him, hurrying to keep up with his pace. Tiled rooftops and darkened gardens emerged from the shadows as they circled the medieval city, climbing up and down steps, skirting the old stone towers. She just prayed that everyone below them was asleep—including don Fernando.

Her pulse quickened at the thought of her patron. Could they really get inside the palace undetected—and into the vault? That was the logical place for don Fernando to keep the necklace—assuming he had it, which she didn't believe. But to reach the vault, they had to dodge guards, motion detectors, video surveillance cameras....

She sucked in a breath, tried to shake off an onrush of nerves. Don Fernando had been fascinated by the necklace, of course. But who hadn't been? The amber was amazing. The center stone was a rare translucent blue, nearly the size of her palm. And the other stones were just as spectacular—black, olive green, deep wine red. And then the occlusions...

A bleak feeling constricted her lungs. What if the thief—or thieves—had removed the stones? The amber itself was priceless. But that necklace... She shivered, remembering the heat in the gold, the power, how it had felt alive in her hands.

As if it really had come from the gods. As if it really had the power to curse someone. As if that ancient legend were true.

And don Fernando had shared her excitement. He'd been as enthralled by it as everyone else. But enough to steal it? To kill for it?

No, she refused to believe that. Not the man who'd been

her patron, who'd acted like a father to her. But now she had to convince Luke of that.

A minute later, they reached a latticed barrier set into an arch—the end of the restored part of the wall. Luke fiddled for a minute, creaked open the makeshift door. "Be careful," he warned her, and stepped through.

She scrambled after him through the narrow doorway, even more alert now. There was no nicely paved path here, just dark, dangerous gaps and crumbling stones. She blocked out thoughts of the necklace, of Luke, concentrated on keeping her balance on the treacherous path. They didn't need another fiasco like they'd had on the roof.

But by the time they reached don Fernando's palace, her pulse was thundering. The scent of roses wafted up from the garden. The moonlight glimmered on the manicured paths. And her footsteps sounded way too loud on the uneven stones, like drumbeats piercing the night.

Luke stopped at the ancient door that led from the wall walk into the compound and checked his watch. He leaned close, and his warm breath brushed her ear. "Three minutes."

Sofia nodded, her tension rising even more. They were timing their entrance to coincide with the guards' shift change. The two men usually stood outside the control room, smoked and chatted for several minutes before the new shift arrived.

And that's when they would go in. But it was going to be tight. Once Luke opened the door, they had exactly sixty seconds to climb down the crumbling stone staircase, cross the garden to the sunroom, and enter the access code on the keypad at the door. One second past that, and the alarm would be triggered, paging the guards. Even before the alarm sounded, a light would show up on the monitors, showing where someone had breached the compound. But Luke intended to disable the system before the incoming guards noticed that.

She clenched her jaw to stop her teeth from clacking. She was wheezing so hard she could barely breathe. She wasn't cut out for a life of crime.

Right on cue, the guards stepped outside. They lit their cigarettes, crunched around the edge of the building to the opposite side. The faint murmur of their voices carried in the still night air.

"Ready?" Luke whispered. She nodded, her pulse hammering against her throat. He beeped the timer on his watch and opened the door.

She scurried after him through the doorway and down the stairs, knowing every second counted. But it was dark, and there wasn't a railing, and she couldn't make out the depths of the steps. She felt her way downward, struggling not to trip, not to skid on the twigs and loose stones, trying to go faster, faster.

The stairs ended abruptly about five feet from the ground. Luke leaped the final distance, then reached back and helped her down.

They tiptoed across the gravel pathway to the grass, raced to the sunroom door. Even so, by the time they got there, she was trembling, tension strangling her gut. How many seconds were left?

She unlatched the keypad beside the door, started to enter her code. She fumbled, hit the wrong button, pressed erase. Luke frowned at his watch. "Ten seconds." She wiped her sweating palms on her jeans, sucked in her breath, started again.

The green light flashed, and relief flooded through her, but she didn't have time to relax. Luke opened the door and hurried her into the building. Now video cameras recorded their movements from every side.

He touched her arm, signaled that he was leaving, and she nodded back. He would disable the system while she searched for the necklace inside the vault. But they had to hurry. Once the guards discovered that the system was down, they would immediately sound the alarm—and the first place they would check would be the vault.

Still shaking, she limped down the hallway to the vault room and punched in the code to unlock the door. Once inside, she snapped on a desk lamp, and its soft haze spread through the room. Then she got to work, checking the steel drawers where the gems were kept. She tried not to worry about the camera in the corner, the motion detectors, about what Luke was doing, the guards…

She opened a drawer with shaking fingers, scanned the contents, closed it again. She searched the next one, then another, working quickly, methodically, but there was no sign of the necklace, just as she'd thought. She was nearly done when she caught a motion at the door and gasped, but it was only Luke. She pressed her hand to her chest to calm her thundering heart.

"Find anything?" he asked, keeping his voice low.

"No," she whispered back. "But I need you to open the safe." That was the one place she couldn't access, where don Fernando kept his most valuable gems.

While Luke went to work on the safe, she checked the last few drawers. He clicked the safe open, and she peered inside.

And saw a red velvet pouch.

Her heart stopped, thudded hard. It wasn't the necklace—the pouch was too small for that. But she recognized that bag, knew exactly what she'd find in it. Fierce dread pounded her lungs.

She reached for it, her hands trembling, and dumped the contents onto her palm. Rare orange and purple sapphires and pigeon's blood rubies tumbled out.

The gems Luke had been accused of stealing five years back.

Their eyes locked. His face turned hard, his gaze dark. Grim lines bracketed his mouth.

And a sick feeling seeped into her heart. So he'd been right. Don Fernando had had those gems all along. She couldn't ignore the proof.

"We need to go," he said, his voice flat. He reset his watch. "Three minutes until the new shift arrives."

She nodded, her movements disjointed as she poured the gems back into the pouch, and set it into the safe. Luke relocked the safe, turned off the lamp, strode from the vault.

She hurried to catch up, but her mind whirled with questions and doubts. So don Fernando had set Luke up. But why? What on earth had he had against Luke? And why had he lied to her?

Her stomach sick, unable to make sense of it all, she trailed Luke back down the hall. They reached the sunroom, stepped into the garden, and she sucked in the cool, morning air. Maybe she'd made a mistake. Maybe the killer had planted those gems there. Maybe—

A door opened across the garden, and light spilled out. Luke grabbed her arm, and they ducked behind a shrub. A second later don Fernando strolled out with Paco—the man who had stolen the necklace and killed Luke's partner. The man who'd probably attacked Luke's aunt.

Her heart plummeted. She'd phoned don Fernando and warned him about his bodyguard, so there was no way he didn't know. Which proved the two men were in this together. His concern for her had been fake. He'd lied to her—now and in the past.

She had trusted the wrong man.

And everything she'd worked for, everything she thought she was, was based on a lie.

The men turned the corner to the control room, disappeared from sight. "Thirty seconds," Luke whispered, his voice terse. "Come on!"

He yanked her from the shrubs, jerked her into motion, and she stumbled after him to the stairs. He heaved himself onto the steps, then reached down and hoisted her up. Her nerves screaming, knowing they had only seconds left, she scrabbled behind him up the stairs to the wall.

Then Luke's watch beeped, and her adrenaline surged. She rushed through the doorway, raced over the wall. They were almost past the palace. Just a few more yards…

Below her, a shout rang out. She stumbled, regained her balance, whipped her head back to see. Guards pounded across the garden toward them, their weapons drawn.

Their time had just run out.

Chapter 10

Fear shrieked through Sofia's mind, freezing her limbs. Run. She had to run. The guards had seen them. They were going to shoot them. They had to get away fast.

"This way," Luke urged, and she yanked her gaze from the guards. He leaped to the stone fence bordering the compound, then down to the ground on the opposite side. It looked far, too far, but there was no other way off the wall.

Then a gun barked, and the bullet cracked the stone near her head. She gasped, not caring about the distance now, leaped to the fence and jumped again. Luke rushed over to break her fall, and she crashed with him to the ground. The force jarred the breath from her lungs.

But Luke rolled to his feet and hauled her upright. And before she could even inhale, they were in motion again, sprinting through the neighbor's garden, plunging through bushes, searching for the fastest way out. They rushed around the side of the house, reached a service entrance, abruptly stopped.

There was no time for finesse or picking locks. Luke kicked the door open, setting off an alarm, and they tumbled onto the street. Sofia glanced toward don Fernando's palace just as that door opened, and her heart made a terrified lurch. But Luke grabbed her arm and jerked her into action again.

She raced with him up the narrow street, veered down an adjacent alley. A shout came from behind them, the pounding of footsteps.

"This way," Luke said, and they changed directions again, dodging parked cars, bolting across a medieval plaza, the uneven cobblestones punishing her feet. Her lungs burned, and her breath rasped. *Hurry, hurry, hurry* hammered her brain.

They wove through the warren of ancient streets, past the Mercado Chico, uphill toward the cathedral and the wall beyond. They lost one of the guards, but another still trailed them, gaining on them, coming closer, closer.

Her lungs heaved. Her breath came in raw, painful gasps. And she knew that she'd never make it. She was exhausted, limping badly. Luke grabbed her arm, forced her to run faster, faster, but she knew she was moving too slow.

They passed a Dumpster, and suddenly, Luke stopped. She stumbled, off-balance, and he pulled her behind it, wedging her down with his weight. She sucked in the stench of garbage, gasped for air. Her heart sped in her chest.

"Stay here," he said.

"What?" Her panic surged. "No! Luke—"

"Shh." Footsteps slapped on the cobblestones, then slowed. The guard. He'd caught up to them. An awful fear jammed in her throat.

Then Luke leaped out from behind the Dumpster, crashed

into the man. They fell, rolled, grunted, scrabbled in a flurry of fists and sickening thuds. Their assailant was big, brawny, but Luke struck back, fighting with a fury she'd never seen.

But then the guard clipped Luke's jaw, and his head snapped back. He crashed against the building, and Sofia stifled a cry. But Luke recovered, flung himself forward, and the two men collided again.

A dull gleam caught her eye, and her heart went berserk. A gun. The guard had a gun! She couldn't let him shoot Luke.

Fear seized her throat, sizzled into her brain. She lunged to her feet, looked around wildly, searching for a board, a rock, anything she could use to save Luke.

But Luke tackled the man, slammed his arm against the pavement, and the pistol skidded away. Her heart thundering, she rushed out and picked it up.

She wheeled around, aimed it at the grappling men. "Stop!"

They ignored her. They were on their feet now, both breathing heavily and circling, but somehow, their assailant had pulled out a knife. The blade glinted ominously in the gray dawn light.

She shifted, raised the gun, but she was shaking too hard to aim straight. She'd never fired a gun before, knew nothing except that she had to pull the trigger. And what if she missed and shot Luke?

"Stop," she cried again. "Stop or I'll shoot!"

Luke spared her a glance, his expression fierce. "Get back!"

She backed up, bumped against the Dumpster, but kept the pistol trained on the guard. Why didn't Luke move? She couldn't risk hitting him. She swallowed, fought down an onrush of nerves. Could she really pull the trigger and shoot a man?

Yes. This man was trying to kill them. And she wouldn't let him succeed.

She steadied her arm, tightened her grip, waited for Luke to get clear.

But then Luke circled closer. She scooted out of his way, trying for a better angle. Her sudden motion distracted the guard, and he glanced up.

It was the break Luke needed. He charged, thrust the guard's arm up, smashed his fist into his jaw. The knife clattered to the street, and the guard slumped down. He hit the stones and lay still.

Sofia gaped at Luke, shocked. How had he learned to fight like that? She tried to swallow, still quivering badly, and lowered the gun. "Is he dead?"

Luke leaned over the man, checked for a pulse. "Just unconscious." He braced his hands on his thighs, and she heard him sucking in air. He glanced at her, his face dark, then scowled. "Give me that gun before you shoot yourself."

He straightened, walked to her, took the weapon from her shaking hands. He checked it, shoved it into the back pocket of his jeans, then strode back and retrieved the knife. "Someone you know?"

Still trembling, she forced herself to scoot close. The man was balding, in his forties, but she didn't know him. She shook her head, hugged her arms. "No, I've never seen him before. He must be new."

But a mark on his neck caught her attention. "Luke, look at that."

"Yeah." He jerked the man's collar open, revealing a tattoo. A crescent moon with a slash across. The same tattoo Antonio had had.

Luke's eyes met hers, and he looked as confused as she felt.

But then a siren wailed, and her pulse thumped hard. Now they had to worry about the police.

"Come on." Luke stepped back, jerked his head. "They'll block off the city next."

He was right. They couldn't stay here. She forced herself to start moving again. But just before they turned the corner, she glanced back at the guard sprawled across the road, and a chill shuddered up her spine. She didn't know what on earth that tattoo meant—but she had a feeling it was bad.

Sofia had finally stopped shaking by the time they parked in a secluded spot in the Sierra de Gredos mountains outside of Ávila. But while her nerves had calmed, she couldn't forget the terrible truth she'd learned about don Fernando. He'd lied to her, deceived her—abused her trust.

And she felt like such a fool. How could she have been so blind about him for so many years? Why hadn't she seen any signs?

And she'd made the same mistake with Luke. She'd thought he'd deceived her, used her—but she had misjudged him, too.

She inhaled the fresh scent of pine, and the irony struck her hard. So here she was, betrayed herself now, her carefully built world torn to shreds. As alone as Luke had been five years ago.

And now she knew exactly how he'd felt.

He emerged from a thick stand of pines. She watched him approach, his muscles flexing beneath his T-shirt, his power obvious in his loose-hipped stride. His black hair glinted in the morning light, and he looked ruthless, dangerous, especially with the dark, gunslinger beard stubble shadowing his jaw. She shivered, remembering how deadly he'd been in that fight.

He was strong, all right, a survivor. He'd refused to give up when his reputation had been destroyed. Even now he kept fighting, despite the odds.

And now she had to follow his example and do the same.

He came closer, and her gaze traveled down his hard, flat stomach to the bloody handkerchief encircling his fist. And she realized that he'd been injured again, probably reopened the cuts from that roof. But they couldn't go to a doctor—at least, not yet.

She inhaled, tried to calm her sudden panic. Would their lives ever get back to normal? Would this nightmare ever end? With every passing hour, it just kept getting worse.

Knowing she couldn't dwell on those fears now, she rummaged in the glove compartment for a rag. At least she could bandage Luke's hand while they made their plans.

She grabbed a bottle of water and climbed out of the car, just as Luke approached the door. "It's clear," he said. "We can rest here for a bit."

"Good." Her calf throbbed. Her eyes felt scratchy from lack of sleep, and she wanted desperately to rest. She slanted him a glance as he grabbed a blanket from the backseat, and marveled again at his endless energy, wondering how he could stay so strong.

She helped him spread the blanket under the trees, then stretched out in the shade and closed her eyes. She breathed in the sweet mountain air, listened to the pine needles swish in the breeze, the rustle of nearby oaks.

Then Luke lowered himself beside her, and she opened her eyes. She traced the corded tendons in his forearms with her gaze, the curve of his biceps beneath his sleeves. Her gaze swept up to his massive shoulders, lingered on the bruise swelling under his eye. Then he turned his head, and his eyes met hers. Memories of that kiss rushed back, and she shivered hard.

Her belly suddenly fluttering, she sat up. "Why don't we bandage that hand?"

He glanced down, frowned at his bloody fist. "I guess." While she busied herself tearing the rag into strips, he grabbed the bottle, leaned away from the blanket, and rinsed his hand.

Then he shifted closer, and his wide shoulder bumped against hers. He held out his hand, and she blotted the callused skin dry, started wrapping his fingers with the cotton rag. She eyed the scrapes marring his knuckles, the dusky skin stretched over his veins, the dark hair that marched up his arm. And she tried not to think about his heat, the scent of his skin, the way his arm brushed against hers. Or exactly how close he was.

She inhaled, tried to focus instead on the necklace and the mess they were in. "What do you think about that tattoo?" she asked.

"Hell if I know. The crescent moon's interesting, though."

"Because it's a Roma symbol, you mean?"

"Yeah." His eyes met hers. "Isn't it on the necklace?"

She nodded. He was right. The moon was a symbol of early Roma culture, along with the serpent and sun. She tied off the first piece of cloth, grabbed another and started wrapping his fingers again.

"But that slash…" She frowned, shook her head. "I've never seen a moon like that. That part's not on the necklace. And I've never seen it on any other antiquity, either."

"Don Fernando never mentioned it?"

"No. But he obviously didn't confide in me." She knotted the cloth, and the hurt, the sense of loneliness flooded through her again, the weight of everything she'd lost. She had no one to turn to now, no job, no home. She was a fugitive from the police, target of a vicious killer, mired in a deadly predicament she didn't understand.

Fear spiraled through her again, and she battled the sudden urge to curl up and close her eyes, make the horror go away.

But she couldn't. There was no rock pile to get lost in this time, no precious gems. For once she had to face reality and fight back.

And not just for her sake. Luke was caught in this, too.

He turned his hand over, capturing hers, and she managed a smile, taking comfort in the strength of his hand, the warmth of his skin. "I know a professor in Salamanca," she said. "I met him at a conference, and we've kept in touch. He's retired now, but he's an expert on ancient symbols. Maybe he can tell us something." She glanced at the sky, tried to ignore the shivers she felt at Luke's touch. "We could go there later if you think it's safe."

His eyes met hers. He seemed nearer somehow, although she hadn't seen him move. "Can we trust him?"

She let out a short, bitter laugh. "How would I know? I trusted don Fernando, remember?"

He let go of her hand, tucked a short strand of hair behind her ear, making her heart beat faster. "It wasn't your fault. He set you up."

She grimaced, feeling foolish again, betrayed. Unable to reconcile reality with the man she knew—or had thought she knew. "I just don't understand it. He helped me. He really did help me, Luke. He got me that internship, gave me so many opportunities, helped me live out my dream."

And now he'd destroyed it. The line between reproduction and forgery was a fine one, and don Fernando had made her an accomplice to a crime. "And why me? That's what I don't get. Why set me up? It doesn't make any sense."

"He set me up, too, remember?"

She could hardly forget it. And that horrible fear slunk through her again, raising goose bumps on her scalp. She rubbed her arms, trying to shake the awful foreboding, the feeling that had been building since Luke's aunt was attacked, that something evil was going on, something bigger than they knew.

"Luke." Her voice wavered. She hesitated, not sure how to say it, or if he'd even believe it. "I have a really bad feeling about this."

"Yeah." His eyes met hers, and she knew that he felt it, too.

He settled his arm around her shoulders, enveloping her in his warmth. Then he tipped up her chin, stroked her jaw with his callused thumb, sending shivers dancing over her skin. "You know, we're going to survive this."

She tried to smile, to take comfort in his assurance, his strength. He was so brave, so fearless.

And so sexy with those dark gold eyes, that sensual mouth. She raised her hand, traced the bruise puffing his battered cheek, the chiseled planes of his face. The black stubble coating his jaw made him look tougher, more masculine. More dangerous.

A thrill shuddered through her.

His eyes darkened, burned into hers. Heat sizzled inside her, and her heart pumped fast.

Later. The promise seared through her again, igniting her nerves. They were alone now, safe. And she needed desperately to forget the danger, the pain.

"Luke," she whispered, her voice raw.

His gaze dropped to her lips, flicked back up, and the stark hunger in his eyes scalded her skin. He slid his hand to her throat, lowered his head. And then his lips were on hers, insistent, igniting, hot.

Exactly as she'd longed for, as she'd dreamed.

His kiss was as rough and potent as he was, sending fierce jolts of pleasure jumping along her nerves. He didn't tease, didn't coax, he simply took, claiming her with his mouth, his tongue, demanding she respond. And she clung to him, lost in the delirious intensity, the fury of need he unleashed.

He growled against her mouth, a deep, masculine sound that sent chills over her skin. His kiss pulled her under, drugging her, and his blatant hunger ignited hers. And she roused to his taste, his scent, to the perfect feel of his lips on hers, the raw urgency of his touch.

He broke the kiss, laid her back against the blanket, his strong body braced above hers. She trailed her fingertips over his bristly jaw, traced the sexy grooves tightening his mouth, plunged her hands through his thick, silky hair.

But then he slanted his mouth over hers, and she forgot to breathe. She thrilled at the warm, male scent of his skin, the brush of his beard stubble caressing her cheek, the weight of his powerful body on hers. She stroked her hands down his back, felt his muscles flex under her palms, his heart beating hard against hers.

And his huge hands roamed everywhere, blazing fire along her hips, her ribs, her breasts. She gasped against his mouth, the erotic feel of him robbing her breath. She couldn't think, could only feel the torrents of pleasure shocking through her. She arched against him and moaned.

He made a low, rough sound of approval. And then his mouth raked over her jaw, her throat, making her pulse go wild, and his ragged breath sawed in her ear. He caught her hand, inched it down his muscled torso to the front of his faded jeans, and the heavy, rigid feel of him halted her lungs.

He lifted his head, and his fevered gaze drilled into hers. Hunger tightened his jaw, turned the planes of his dark face taut. And she gazed up at him, riveted by the need, the heat. The stark honesty in his eyes.

The connection she'd felt so long ago.

Her breath hitched. A fierce rush of desire scalded her nerves.

He rose to his knees, stripped off her clothes then paused. And for an endless moment he just looked at her, his gaze devouring every intimate inch of her, his eyes rapt, intent. The muscles deep in her belly throbbed in response.

The cool breeze gusted, rippling over her skin, and she shivered, feeling exposed. She lifted her arms to cover herself, but he captured her wrists and blocked the move, pressed her arms back over her head. And he studied her, his gaze stroking up and down her bare flesh, as if she were an intricate lock he intended to pick. Then his eyes turned hotter yet.

"You're so damn beautiful," he said, his voice raw.

He was wrong. But he made her feel beautiful—wanted, desired. And she realized that she'd always loved that about him, how he'd made her feel unique, as if he'd truly wanted *her,* not just her skill with the stones.

"Do you know how many nights I've dreamed of this?" he rasped.

His admission caught her off guard. She parted her lips, wanting to answer, but her throat felt too thick to speak. Luke had thought of her, dreamed of her—despite the past, despite the pain.

His eyes turned even more predatory, and he reclaimed her mouth, released her wrists. And his callused hands skimmed everywhere—her belly, her thighs, her breasts.

And then his mouth replaced his hands, and she moaned. Need edged out want, burning through her blood.

"Luke." Her voice was a throaty plea.

He raised his head. His eyes trapped hers, and the raw heat in them made her heart pound. Molten gold, fused by fire. The color she'd always loved most. And then he tore off his clothes, his gaze never wavering from hers.

And the masculine beauty of him washed over her again, halting her breath. He was glorious—totally male, all roped tendons and muscled strength, blatantly aroused.

And he wanted her. Wanted *her.* Not the amber expert, not the elegant role she played, but the real her, the woman with insecurities and doubts and fears.

Then he lowered himself to her, urged her legs apart and slowly, deliriously drove inside her—hard, heavy, hot. Filling her, claiming her, possessing her. And she welcomed this amazing man home.

Perfect. He was perfect. His gaze smoldered into hers, dark, sensual, driven by hunger and heat. His urgency fueled hers, tearing a ragged groan from her throat, driving her higher yet. Lashing her with pleasure, torturing her with heat. And she felt that connection with him again. The intimacy. The love.

The truth of that slammed through her. She still loved him. She'd never stopped.

The words bubbled inside her, but she bit them back, knowing he wasn't ready to hear them now. The discovery was too fragile, too fresh, too raw.

And then he kissed her again, fusing his mouth to hers in an urgent, carnal kiss that made her forget to think. And her need for him turned frantic, the craving expanding, until she was frenzied, desperate, until finally, finally, the hunger exploded in bliss.

And she clung to him, coming again and again as he pumped into her, splintering, convulsing, crying out as the ecstasy raged.

And he shuddered, groaned, until slowly, inevitably, the world stopped moving, and she opened her eyes. And then she hugged him, tears brimming in her eyes, a huge swell of emotion crowding her throat. He was perfect, so perfect. She clung to him, thrilled at his harsh breath rasping in her ear, his heart thundering against her chest. Relishing the feel of him pulsing inside her, the aftershocks of pleasure still bursting in her veins.

She wanted to laugh, weep from the wild emotions coursing through her. This man meant everything to her, always had. He was the only one who'd understood her, the only one who'd really cared.

But then he withdrew, rolled off her, his eyes not quite

meeting hers. He glanced at his watch, stood, and a chill crept over her heart.

He pulled on his clothes, his movements brusque, and his silence weighed on her, draining the remnants of pleasure from her blood. Disbelief swept through her, morphed into hurt, and then an awful ache invaded her chest. He was retreating, pulling away.

Rejecting her?

"We'll eat, then head to Salamanca to talk to that guy you know," he finally said, still not looking her way.

Misery spiraled through her, sinking to the pit of her gut. She'd been wrong, totally wrong. That had just been sex. He really didn't love her back.

Feeling awkward, exposed, foolish, she grabbed her bra, her shirt, and tugged them on. Then she stumbled to her feet and jerked on her jeans. So she'd only imagined that connection. She had misjudged him again.

And she'd thought things couldn't get worse.

She pulled on her shoes, fought down the pain. Of course, he'd never said that he loved her—only desired her, which wasn't the same thing at all.

And she couldn't let him see how much that hurt. Or what a fool she'd been—again.

She sucked in her breath, pieced together her pride. "You go ahead." She struggled to sound casual, normal. "I'm not hungry right now."

He turned around then, and his eyes met hers. And she saw the distance, the regret. "Sofia…"

No, she couldn't deal with this now. "I'll be back in a minute. I need to…you know." She motioned toward the pine trees, backed up.

"Sofia, listen. It's not—" he began, but she whirled around and hurried away.

Desperate for privacy, unwilling to break down in front of him, she hobbled through the trees, feeling shredded, rejected, sick. Needing to get away, lick her wounds, think.

She rounded a boulder, dragged in a breath. She wished she could blame don Fernando for this fiasco—he'd lied to her, ruined her relationship with Luke, caused her to turn against him in the past.

But as she stumbled over the rocky ground, she realized she couldn't do it. Not anymore. She had to be honest for once.

She stopped by a stream, pressed her palm to her chest and forced herself to think back. Five years ago, Luke had loved her. She was positive she hadn't misjudged that. She'd felt it in his kiss, the way he'd made love to her. That connection she'd felt had been real.

But then she'd wrecked it. She'd been scared and insecure, desperate for acceptance. And as a result, she'd sided with the wrong man.

So this was her fault. She had destroyed Luke's love. She'd made her choices back then—bad ones, but she was to blame.

And now she had to live with that fact.

Or did she? She knelt awkwardly beside the gurgling stream, splashed cold water on her face, then stopped. Was it really too late to win Luke back? Because for a moment there, when he'd been inside her... She'd thought for sure she'd seen love in his eyes.

But maybe she was deluding herself again, confusing lust with love. She'd been wrong about everything else.

She finished washing her face, smoothed back her hair. And she realized that if there was any chance he still had feelings for her, she had to try.

But how?

She hadn't believed him before. So now she had to convince

him that he could trust her, that she didn't doubt him, that she'd stick by him no matter what. But how could she do that?

By bringing down don Fernando. She had to help Luke find that necklace, expose the truth, restore the honor he'd lost—the honor she'd unwittingly helped destroy.

Of course, she would forever obliterate her career in the process. Just clearing her own name was one thing. Revealing don Fernando's guilt was much worse. No one would hire the protégée of a murdering thief.

And without her art, without her career...

A lifetime of rejections and insecurities crashed in on her, and she pressed her hand to her throat. Her work was more than just a career to her. It was her identity, her path to acceptance, her dream.

But acceptance without integrity didn't mean much. And she couldn't base her life on a lie.

Especially if it hurt the man she loved.

She rose, pulled in her breath. So her path was clear. She had to vindicate Luke, earn back his trust.

And take the biggest risk of her life.

Because if she was wrong, if he didn't love her back, she'd lose more than her career. She would end up with nothing at all.

Chapter 11

He'd acted like a jerk. He'd hurt Sofia's feelings, frozen her out after the most phenomenal sex of his life and behaved like a self-centered ass.

Disgusted at himself, Luke strode down a narrow side street off the Plaza Mayor in Salamanca, sweating in the rising heat. He'd had to create some distance between them, no doubt about that. He'd had to shut down, keep himself from saying something he might later regret. Because no matter how great the sex was, no matter if he now believed her, no matter how perfectly right she'd felt in his arms, he refused to get that involved, be that vulnerable to anyone again.

He spotted her sitting on a bench in the shade, pigeons pecking nearby. She tipped her head up and sipped from a bottle of water, exposing the creamy sweep of her throat. His gaze dropped to her breasts, and he instantly flashed back to the erotic feel of her, all ripe, welcoming curves and soft flesh.

A hard rush of lust jolted his body, and he hissed at the unruly need. *Phenomenal* didn't begin to describe that experience. She'd been incredible, better than he'd remembered, better than any fantasy he'd ever had. And every sigh, every move, every moist, warm, silky inch of her had been forever scorched into his brain.

And it had taken more self-control than he'd thought he'd had to keep from reaching for her again, to get up from that blanket and turn away.

He dodged a cluster of tourists blocking the sidewalk, still keeping his eye on Sofia. She glanced up, spotted him, and nervously tucked her hair behind her ear. And even the dark sunglasses she now wore couldn't hide the hurt, the uncertainty on her beautiful face.

And his opinion of himself sank even lower. Maybe he'd had to retreat, but he should have handled it better. Because the truth was, no matter how much he wanted to keep his distance, he really did care about her. He couldn't help it. He understood her lonely childhood, the hurt she felt over being betrayed—more than she could know. And he respected her courage now.

But he still couldn't let himself need her again.

And that was the real problem—the overwhelming need that swamped him when he'd taken her into his arms. He'd been too tempted to lose himself in that warmth and let himself trust her again.

So he'd pulled back—badly, but it had had to be done. And now he needed to keep that distance. He had to concentrate on finding that necklace, restore his honor, his name.

And keep his hands off Sofia.

But he also had to explain, apologize for his freezing act. He knew he owed her that much. But that would have to wait for a better time.

"How's your aunt?" she asked when he got close.

He sat down on the concrete bench, putting enough space between them to keep from reaching for her again. "Better. She's been downgraded from critical to serious."

"That's good."

"Yeah. They think she'll survive." No thanks to him. He shook his head in disgust, exhaled, and more guilt piled up in his chest.

He'd put her in danger, all right. And now they were about to do the same thing to someone else, this professor Sofia knew. She held out the bottle of water, and he took it, slugged the cool liquid down. They didn't have much choice, though. They needed to find that necklace, and that tattoo was their only clue.

He took another gulp of water, scowled at the pigeons strutting over the cobblestones in search of crumbs and flicked his gaze to the tourists milling nearby. He just hoped they could trust this professor. He finished off the water, recapped the plastic bottle, tapped it on his thigh.

But one thing was sure. With the danger they were in, he had to stay alert—and not let anyone, even Sofia, distract him.

"You ready?" he asked.

She nodded, and he rose, tossed the empty bottle into a trash can, wiped his forehead on his sleeve. The old city baked in the August heat, even at this early hour, but that was fine with him. The locals usually headed north for the month, leaving the city to tourists and foreign students—who were far less likely to follow the news.

"You think this professor's still in the city?" he asked as they started walking.

"He should be. I think he still teaches a summer class."

They worked their way through the maze of cobblestone streets, past the university to the professor's apartment, a fifteenth-century building that had been renovated inside. Luke kept watch on the deserted street while Sofia rang his third-floor apartment. *"¿Sí?"* a man answered on the intercom.

"Professor Ortiz? It's Sofia. Sofia Mikhelson."

There was a pause. Luke's eyes met hers, and she nibbled her bottom lip. They'd better be able to trust this man.

"Entra," the professor said and buzzed them in.

Luke glanced around to make sure no one saw them, then ushered her inside. He stayed close to her, his hand on the small of her back, as they rode the elevator to the third floor.

Professor Ortiz answered his door on their first knock. He was a short, thick man, close to seventy, with a full gray beard and receding hair. Dark eyebrows shot with gray framed wary, intelligent eyes.

And Luke knew instantly that this man recognized him, had followed their story in the news. But the question remained: Could they trust him?

"Sofia." The professor turned smoothly back to Sofia. "This is a surprise." Sofia stepped forward and kissed him on both cheeks.

"I'm sorry to involve you in this," she said as soon as they'd stepped inside and the professor had closed the door. "It's all been a terrible mistake. We haven't done anything wrong. We really haven't. I hope you don't mind that we came here. We thought that you could help."

The professor frowned, skipped his gaze to Luke and back. "Of course, I'm happy to help you. But I'm not sure what I can do."

"We just need information about a symbol," she assured him. "We think it might help us find the missing necklace."

If he was surprised, he didn't show it. "Certainly. Come in." He motioned them into a small library crammed with bookcases. More books littered the floor. "Sit, please." He gestured toward two armchairs that flanked a massive desk. "Would you like something to drink?"

"No, gracias," Luke said. He didn't trust the guy yet, didn't want him out of their sight.

When Sofia shook her head, the professor shrugged, took a seat at the desk. "So, tell me. What symbol do you need to know about?"

"The crescent moon," Sofia said.

"The crescent moon…" The professor took off his glasses, pulled a cloth from the desk, began methodically polishing the lenses. "Of course, you know it's a Roma symbol." He glanced at Luke. "You're Calé?"

Luke shrugged. He could hardly deny his Gypsy heritage, plus it had been on the news.

"Then you know the Roma history?"

"That they came from India, you mean?"

The professor nodded. "In the eleventh century. They were warriors, members of the Kshatriya caste, descended from the sun and moon." He looked at Sofia. "You saw those symbols on the necklace?"

"Yes, but…" She hesitated, glanced at Luke, and he knew she was choosing her words. "We also saw the moon on a tattoo. It was a black crescent moon with a diagonal slash. We wondered if it might be connected to the necklace somehow."

The professor stilled, then slowly resumed cleaning his glasses. The pause was brief, hardly noticeable, but Luke caught the tremor in his hands, the sudden pallor in his face. "So you recognize it," Luke said.

"There were rumors once.…" The professor cleared his throat, put his glasses on. And Luke knew they'd shaken the man. "But that was a long time ago. I doubt they're true."

"What kind of rumors?" he pressed.

"It was years ago, back in my own university days. I hadn't been in Salamanca long. The rumors were all hushed up, of course, very secretive, but that just increased the appeal."

The professor glanced away, as if lost in thought, then flicked his gaze back to Luke. "The symbol was used by a secret society called the Order of the Black Crescent Moon."

"A secret society?" Sofia said, sounding stunned.

He gave her an apologetic smile. "The symbol interested me because of its connection to the Roma legend."

"So there is a connection?"

"Yes. The color black represents the Hindu goddess Kali, also known as Parvati."

"Saint Sarah," Luke murmured. "The Romani goddess of fate."

"Yes, exactly right." The professor nodded his approval. "Different names for the same goddess. The crescent moon stands for her consort, Shiva, a Hindu icon of masculinity. So you have both feminine and masculine elements. The moon also signifies time—past, present, future."

"And the slash?" Sofia asked.

"That would be Shiva's trident, which represents power over all things."

"Ambitious society," Luke said.

The professor shrugged. "Supposedly, it was formed in the eleventh century by a king who'd descended from the ancient Sumerians. He believed that he was the rightful owner of the three treasures, not the Gypsies. He claimed the Gypsies stole them from him. So he formed the society to get them back. At least that was the rumor. The society's existence was never confirmed."

Luke stared at him, sure he had to be joking. "But that's crazy. The legend's a myth."

"You're familiar with it?"

"Who isn't?" Not only had it been publicized in the news since the necklace was found, but it was a standard Gypsy tale. The warrior goddess Parvati, impressed with a Roma king's courage in battle, rewarded him with three sacred possessions—a necklace, dagger, and crown—which, combined, gave him the power to rule the earth. But then a hotheaded prince rose to the throne, lusted after a virgin who'd been promised to another man, and used those powers to take her. Distraught, disgraced, she stabbed herself in the heart. But before she died, she cursed the king and condemned the Gypsies to roam.

And promised that only when a worthy Roma leader emerged would the three treasures finally be reunited—an event that would be foreshadowed by a blood-red lunar eclipse.

Luke eyed the swell of Sofia's breasts, the seductive line of her throat. Hell, the young king's lust was the only part of the legend that made any sense. Desire that strong could drive a man to desperate acts, make him lose all control.

He'd certainly lost his around Sofia.

"It's a fairy tale," he said. "It isn't true."

Sofia frowned. "I'm not so sure."

"Oh, come on." He stared at her in disbelief. "You can't be serious."

"There are a lot of legends in the antiquities world," she said. "Everyone loves the idea of hidden treasure. But this one's been around for centuries. And whenever a legend lasts that long, there's usually some truth to it, some reason it began.

"The necklace checked out," she continued before he could argue. "Tests date it to the eleventh century. The gold is the same carat, same purity mined in northwest India at the time. And we know the amber route from the Baltic was in full use then. That's well documented from both Eastern and Western sources."

"So the necklace is Roma. That doesn't mean the legend's true."

"No, but historical data support it. We know the Roma came from northwest India. They were warriors, captured by Muslims—"

"Because they lost a battle, not because they'd been cursed."

"Right. But even if the legend is fiction, it's supported by facts." She held up her hand to tick them off. "The Gypsies were driven out of India. They've been forced to roam ever since—whether it's because of a curse or not doesn't change history. And now one of the rumored treasures has turned up, supporting the legend even more."

He shot her a look of disbelief. "So it follows that there's a curse? That the necklace has special powers?"

"No, of course not. But you said your aunt believes it."

"Yeah."

"And if your aunt believes it, others do, too."

He exhaled. She had a point. And he had seen those tattoos. But a secret society? *Hombre.* The world had gone mad.

Sofia looked at the professor again. "What else do you know about this society?"

"Not much." The professor rose from his chair, strolled to the balcony window. "There's an inner circle, the knights. Those are the ones with the tattoos. The other members of the society are soldiers."

"Soldiers?" Sofia wrinkled her forehead. "What do they do?"

"They study, search old documents and artwork looking for clues, try to recover the missing treasures."

Luke could see the appeal. An obscure legend. Priceless treasures. The lure of ancient powers.

But this wasn't a game. People had died because of this Black Crescent society—if it really existed. And unless they were careful, Sofia could be next.

A restless, uneasy feeling pulsed through him at that thought. He stood, paced to the bookcase and back, trying to shake it, to calm himself down. But a rumble of urgency plucked at his nerves, just as it had at his aunt's.

His eyes met Sofia's, and he jerked his head toward the door.

She nodded, rose. "We'd better go." She faced the professor again. "Thank you so much. You've been a huge help. At least now we have something to go on."

"What do you plan to do?"

She shrugged. "Find the necklace if we can. Try to prove that we didn't steal it."

The professor frowned. "This secret society... You realize it could be dangerous if it exists. Have you contacted the police?"

She glanced at Luke, and he shook his head, silently reminding her not to mention don Fernando. "Not yet," she said. "I'm sure you've seen the news. They already think we're guilty."

"Still..." The professor moved back to his desk, jotted something on a business card, handed it to her. "My sister's husband. He's with the *Guardia Civil* here in Salamanca. I'm sure he'll help you."

Sofia looked at the card. "You think we can trust him?"

"He's an honest man, fair. Tell him I said to call."

She nodded, slipped the card into the pocket of her jeans. "Thank you."

"You're quite welcome." He stretched out his hand, escorted them to the door.

But just before he went through the doorway, Luke realized that the professor had left something out. Something important.

He paused, glanced at the professor again. "You never said. How do the members of this society become knights?"

"They pass a test—a test of loyalty. At a ceremony, when the moon is full."

"And the test?"

The professor's gaze locked on his. And suddenly, a chill crawled over Luke's skin, and the hairs on his nape stood on end. Unease whispered through him again, filling him with foreboding, urgency, dread.

"They murder a Gypsy." The professor's gaze shifted to Sofia. "And anyone who tries to stop them."

Chapter 12

"So what do you think?" Sofia asked, sounding nervous. Luke held open the lobby door for her, then followed her into the midday heat. What he thought was that he needed to get her out of this place, get her to safety fast. Because that bombshell the professor just dropped had unnerved him. And he couldn't silence the sense of danger that hammered inside his skull.

The skin still prickled on the back of his neck. He snapped his gaze to the professor's apartment, saw a shadow by the third story window move.

His heart stilled. So the professor had been watching them leave. What did that mean? Or was he getting paranoid now?

He frowned, caught up with Sofia. "I don't know," he said, answering her question. "The whole thing sounds bizarre."

"But we did see those tattoos."

"Yeah." Those tattoos made it impossible to shrug the society off. And if it really existed…

Another sliver of unease crawled through him. Fighting the bodyguard was hard enough. But protecting Sofia from an entire organization…

He moved closer to her, instinctively prodding her into the narrow strip of shade cast by the medieval buildings. In the distance, church bells clanged, their discordant notes jarring his already edgy nerves.

He couldn't trust anyone else to guard her—he knew that much. The attack on his aunt proved that he needed to keep her close. But taking her with him while he searched for that necklace could be an even greater risk.

But did he have a choice? They turned the corner, headed down the pedestrian-only street that led back to the Plaza Mayor. He scanned the handful of tourists trekking past in the sweltering heat, the flock of pigeons scouring the cobblestones in search of crumbs.

And that insistent feeling that something bad was going to happen kept drumming through his head.

"Do you think we should call that *guardia?*" Sofia asked.

"I don't know." He blew out his breath, plunged his bandaged hand through his hair. He didn't know much of anything right now—what to do with Sofia, where the necklace was, why don Fernando had left his palace this morning, or where he'd gone.

"I'm thinking we should call him." She hesitated. "I mean, what if we find the necklace? How are we going to prove that we didn't steal it? Maybe if we have the police on our side, if we tell the professor's brother-in-law what we're doing…"

"Maybe." He still didn't trust the professor, and he sure didn't trust the police. Generations of prejudice against Gypsies, plus his own bad experiences guaranteed that. But she was right. This situation was deadly. They'd be safer if they had someone with authority on their side.

And assuming that this society existed—and he was starting to believe that it did—then they might not be the only ones involved here. Other innocent lives could be at risk.

But damn, he didn't like this. His instincts balked at relying on someone unknown. But if he hoped to keep Sofia safe, did he have a choice?

He spotted a pay phone near a bar, stopped again. "Let me see that card."

She pulled it from her pocket and handed it over. He fingered the card, thought hard, glanced at his watch. Then he handed it back. "All right." They'd take the chance and contact this *guardia*. "But we're going to do this my way. I don't want to walk into a trap.

"I want you to call, talk to him directly," he continued. "Tell him we'll meet him at the Plaza Mayor in exactly ten minutes, in front of the *ayuntamiento*." He didn't want to give the guy time to organize backup. "Tell him to come alone, that if he doesn't show up on time, we'll leave. Don't say anything else. If he presses you for information, hang up."

He dug a coin from his pocket, handed it to her. Then, while she limped over to the pay phone, he scanned the street and made plans. The Plaza Mayor was a huge, ancient square enclosed on all four sides by three-story buildings. The *ayuntamiento*, or city hall, formed the north side of the plaza. The street they were on approached from the south.

Sofia walked back. "He said he'd be there. He's wearing a white polo shirt, dark slacks."

"Good." Luke took her arm, strolled with her toward the plaza, keeping their pace slow to blend in with the tourists. But he stayed alert, watching for signs of police activity, while that dull thrum of anxiety rapped at his nerves.

"We'll stay under the portico when we get to the plaza," he continued. "We won't be as visible that way. I want to watch until the *guardia* shows, make sure he's alone." He handed her several more euros. "If we need to look busy, buy something touristy."

A minute later, they reached the deep, arched entrance to the ancient plaza. Luke pulled her to a stop at a souvenir store and pretended to examine the T-shirts on an outside rack. So far he hadn't seen any police, nothing suspicious. It was a typical, tranquil day.

So why did he feel so nervous?

"Okay, let's go," he said, his voice low. "But stay alert." He slowed his breath, strolled beside her through the shadowed entrance. Once inside the plaza, they skirted the open, sunny center, staying close to the buildings in the portico's shade. They passed café tables crowded with tourists, a noisy bar, a pharmacy closed up for the sizzling month.

He scanned the tourists at the tables, the *ayuntamiento* across the plaza, the red and gold flags on its balcony dangling listlessly in the heat. Then a man stepped out from the shadowed arches, and Luke tugged Sofia to a stop. Dark slacks. White shirt.

"That's him."

She looked toward the man. "It looks like he's alone."

"Maybe." He motioned toward a nearby souvenir shop. "We can watch from there."

He followed her into the shop, then positioned himself by the window, pretending to browse through a book while he watched. The *guardia* still stood by the *ayuntamiento*. The man checked his watch, turned to admire an attractive woman sauntering past, nodded to someone nearby.

Luke's heart stopped. He put down the book, shifted to a pile of T-shirts to get a better view. Two men strode past the *guardia*, sat at a café table behind him, and looked around— far too casually.

Undercover cops. So the *guardia* hadn't come alone.

He glanced back to check on Sofia, but she waited at the cash register while the clerk rang someone up. Luke moved close to a rack of key chains, shifted his gaze to the *ayunta-miento*, spotted men hunkered by the belfry on the roof.

He swore. The *guardia* hadn't just called for backup. He'd brought in the whole damned army. So much for trusting the guy.

Sofia came over a second later, lifted her bag. "I got a calendar."

"Great." He glanced at the clerk. The man had moved to one of the shelves lining the wall and was busy straightening some cups. "He brought company," he murmured. "We need to get out of here."

He took her arm, hurried her out the door, headed back toward the arched entrance they'd come through.

But then Sofia stopped. "Luke, wait," she whispered, and he looked up. A cop car pulled into the plaza and blocked their way.

Damn. He ducked his head, jerked Sofia around. Now what? They were trapped in the plaza, the exits blocked. There was no way out unless—

A door opened next to the bar, and a woman stepped out. Luke dropped Sofia's arm and leaped forward, caught the door before it closed. He motioned to Sofia, urged her inside. The heavy door clicked shut behind him, muffling the plaza's noise.

He glanced around. They were beneath the plaza's apartments in a dim, musty lobby lit only by the transom window above the door. A worn wooden staircase led to the upper floors.

"Do you think we can get out the back?" Sofia's voice sounded hollow in the muffled gloom.

"No, these old buildings only have one door. We'll have to hide." The question was *where*. He blew out his breath, thought fast. The city would be flooded with police now, the narrow streets around the plaza blocked. Which meant they had to sit tight until the police gave up.

He just hoped they didn't bring in dogs or the GEO—the Spanish special forces.

He scanned the lobby, located the mailboxes along one wall. He strode to the boxes, pulled out an old lock pick he'd found at his aunt's apartment, opened the first one up.

"What are you doing?" Sofia asked.

"I'm looking to see who's on vacation."

She frowned at him. "You want to hide in somebody's house?"

"We won't stay long. Just until the police are gone." He closed the box, checked another. On the fourth try, he found one stuffed with mail. He shut the flap, glanced at the number on the outside. "One-C. Come on." He loped up the creaking stairs.

Apartment C was one story up at the end of a dingy hall. He opened the front door without problems, ushered Sofia inside. The apartment was stuffy, dark and reeked of stale cigarette smoke, but at least they were safe for now.

He crossed the darkened living room to the balcony window, edged the closed shutter aside. Uniformed police swarmed the plaza, and he swore. They never should have called that *guardia*.

Sofia joined him at the window, peeked through another slat. He heard her suck in her breath. "They're all over the place now."

"Yeah." Disgusted, he dropped the shutter into place. "We might as well get comfortable. We might be here for a while."

Her gaze stayed on his for a moment. And he caught the

fear lurking in those smoky green eyes, the anxious pull of her lips. Then she hobbled to the sofa, her limp suddenly more pronounced.

That was his fault, too. He'd worn her out, put that fear in her eyes, embroiled them in a terrible mess.

Because that's what this was, a fiasco. The police had far more resources than don Fernando—more men, helicopters—and they wouldn't give up. They'd scour the city, bring in more forces, block off the roads….

But that wasn't the worst of it. Getting arrested, being jailed for crimes they didn't commit would be bad enough. But the danger went deeper than that—much deeper. Don Fernando had power, connections, even within the police. And no way would he risk letting Luke and Sofia tell the truth—especially now that they knew about that secret society.

Which meant that if they got arrested, they'd be dead.

He blew out his breath, thoroughly disgusted with himself. He hadn't just failed to protect Sofia, he'd endangered her more.

And he knew one thing. He'd never again ignore his instincts.

Still appalled at the disaster he'd landed them in, he trailed her to the sofa. She sank into the sagging cushions, let out a moan and closed her eyes.

He was tempted to do the same. He sat down beside her, let his head drop back. Fatigue rolled through him, a bone-deep exhaustion from the stress, the long hours they'd spent on the run. But he didn't dare sleep. Instead, he turned his mind to the streets around the plaza, determined to figure out how to escape.

"How long do you think before they give up?" Sofia asked a moment later.

"I don't know." Although he doubted it would be soon. But

he wouldn't let her worry about that. "We can sneak out when it gets dark."

She frowned, subsided into silence again. He rubbed the dull ache hammering his temples, fought the drugging pull toward sleep.

"Luke." She hesitated and her eyes met his. "I'm so sorry about the professor. I really am. I thought for sure we could trust him."

"Forget it."

"I can't believe that he tricked us. He helped me get work, invited me to his home, introduced me to people he knew. I thought he was a friend."

He heard the pain in her voice, the remorse. "Hey, we'll be fine. The police will give up in a while, and then we'll go."

"But what if they don't?" Her voice wobbled. "I know it sounds crazy, but I keep thinking about Antonio, your aunt, and I keep wondering—what if the legend's true, and there really is a curse?"

"That's ridiculous."

"Is it?" Misery tinged her soft voice. "Antonio touched the necklace. He wasn't Roma, and according to the legend, any *payo* who touches it dies." Her eyes met his, her fear palpable. "And he did die."

And he knew what she was thinking. That she had touched it, too.

"Listen." He leaned closer, grasped her chin, felt her tremble under his hand. "Nothing's going to happen to you." He wouldn't allow it. "The curse had nothing to do with his death. He was killed out of greed, a fight between thieves."

"But your aunt believes it, doesn't she? That's why she didn't want me there. She had that premonition. She knew I'd bring danger. And then she got attacked—"

"My aunt's a superstitious old woman. She thinks anyone

who's not a Gypsy brings bad luck. Hell, she's so worried about the evil eye that she hardly leaves the house."

"But—"

"But that's all that curse is, a superstition. Rumors started by the Gypsies to get their necklace back."

She nodded, attempted a smile, but doubt still shadowed her eyes. And something inside his chest moved. She was scared and in pain, exhausted after the past three days. And yet she was trying to be brave.

"Come here." Wanting to reassure her, he slid his arm around her shoulders and pulled her close. She slipped her arms around his waist, rested her head against his chest, and her soft body curved into his. He stroked her back, massaged her neck, just held her, until slowly, gradually, the tension in her body eased.

But a whole different tension began rising in his. "We're going to be all right," he said, his voice husky now.

"Do you really think so?"

"Yeah." He fingered a silky strand of her hair, tucked it behind her ear. His gaze dropped from her cheeks to the sweet, soft swell of her lips. And he knew that he'd better let go.

But she lifted her head, and her eyes trapped his. And before he could stop himself, he dipped his head, slid his lips over hers. He meant the kiss to be soft, comforting, light.

But her scent filled his head. The warmth of her lips lured him in. And then his mind banked down, instincts took over, and the kiss grew deeper, harder, more carnal.

An eternity later, he managed to drag his mouth from hers. His breath sawed in the quiet room. His blood hammered through his skull.

And he stifled a groan. What was it about this woman? One touch, one kiss, and he lost control. Her effect on him was instant, explosive.

But this wasn't the time for sex. He had to plan their escape, watch for the police. Plus, she was exhausted, emotionally drained. And hadn't he vowed to keep his distance?

But damn, he wanted her. He lowered his arms, tipped his head back against the sofa and closed his eyes, trying to ignore how close she was, fighting the hot, vivid memories tormenting his brain. Her velvet skin. That ripe, sultry flesh—all slick and hot and wet. The way her breasts filled his hands, heavy and lush, the way the nipples pebbled under his palms.

Every muscle in his body clenched, and he shifted to ease the ache.

Then she slid closer, turned into his arms. "Luke," she whispered, and his pulse jerked. She feathered kisses along his jaw, laved the bruise by his eye with her tongue, surrounded him with her scent, her touch. He balled his hands, fought the urge to stroke her breasts, her skin, to sink into that glorious warmth, make her vision turn blurry with need.

His gaze caught hers. Her eyes softened, darkened. Fire flared low in his gut.

"Luke, hold me," she whispered, and his blood turned hot. Hell, he was only human. Was it wrong to take pleasure at a time like this?

He tried to beat through the haze muddling his brain, remember why this was wrong. "I can't promise—"

"I know that." She kissed his jaw, his ear, igniting a rush of lust in his blood. "But I just…need you. I want you."

Hell, yes. He shuddered hard. Then he plunged his hands through her hair, pulled her head down to his, gave in to the pounding need. He ravished her mouth—invading, demanding, devouring. No tenderness, no finesse, just urgent, primal lust.

And she kissed him back, her need fueling his, the conflagration mutual, explosive, raw.

A groan rose deep in his throat. A thought sliced through his brain that this was wrong, wrong, wrong. But she felt exactly right. She always had. And he'd worry about that danger later on.

Chapter 13

Bells clanged in the plaza's belfry, the metallic sound pulling Sofia reluctantly back to awareness. She cracked open her eyes, battled the desire to slide back into oblivion, into those glorious dreams of Luke—his insistent hands, that frantic heat...

She clutched the afghan closer to her chin, squinted across the dark apartment. He stood at the balcony window, barefoot and shirtless, the soft haze of a nearby floor lamp casting a sheen on his muscled back.

So it hadn't been a dream.

Her eyes fluttered closed, and she sighed, letting herself sink into the memories again, the sound of his deep, drugging voice, the wicked heat of his mouth. Pleasure skipped through her veins, and she shivered, wanting him again. If only they had more time. If only they didn't have to hide. If only they could make the danger go away.

Luke was an incredible lover. A complicated one.

And she had no idea how he'd react to what they'd done.

Time to find out. She sighed, pulled the afghan closer around her bare body, and rose. He glanced back, then watched her as she approached him, his eyes dark, intent. His gaze never wavered from hers.

She joined him at the window and parted the slats on the blinds, needing a minute to decide what to say. The plaza was mostly deserted now, although police still milled around. A few workers hosed down the pavement. Sanitation trucks removed trash, while other trucks supplied the bars.

"What time is it?" she finally asked, her voice still rusty from sleep.

His gaze stayed on hers. "Four in the morning."

"You're kidding." She blinked. "Wow. I slept for what, about fifteen hours?"

"You needed it."

She couldn't deny that. Even now, exhaustion pulsed through her head, making her eyes burn, weighting her limbs. But they didn't have time to relax. "It looks like the police are still there."

"Yeah. They're organizing a search. We'll have to leave soon."

"Any idea where we can go?"

"Not yet." He didn't say anything more, just watched her. The awkward silence stretched, and disappointment crept through her gut. If she'd hoped for more kisses and whispered words of love, she'd deluded herself.

But she'd vowed not to run from reality again, and she met his gaze straight on. "Morning-after regrets?"

The corner of his mouth quirked up, and the sexy gleam in his eyes made her blood heat. "It's hard to regret something that good."

"Yes." She shivered again, amazed that just the sound of

his voice could arouse her, make her want him all over again. His gaze traveled boldly down her body, her breasts, and she was helpless to resist the pull, the need, the way her body softened for his.

She tightened her hold on the afghan, tempted to let the cloth slide from her hands, to give in to the explosion between them. But he hadn't really answered her question. And behind the hunger in his eyes, the heat, she saw something that looked a lot like remorse.

She pulled her gaze from his, pretended to peer through the slats again, giving herself time to compose herself. "You know…" She struggled to keep her voice even. "If you remember, I was the one who suggested sex. And I didn't ask for a ring."

Silence pulsed through the room. "You're saying that was casual?" he finally said, his voice strangely neutral.

"No." She sighed, dropped the slat, shook her head. She couldn't pretend, not with Luke. "I don't think that…being with you could ever be casual. I just mean that I didn't expect a commitment."

His eyes stayed on hers for a long moment, dark, unreadable, and he looked so rumpled and sexy that her heart rolled. "I wish I could give you one," he said. Regret tinged his voice, and her heart twisted, the dull ache seeping into her throat. She hadn't expected a declaration from him, but a part of her had hoped.…

"I can't lie to you, Sofia. I won't—can't—make a commitment. It's just not in me, not anymore. Maybe it never was."

Because she'd ruined it. Her heart faltered, and that desolate feeling settled again in her lungs. He didn't have to say the words to remind her. She'd destroyed his love years back.

"Things like loyalty, love…" He folded his powerful arms across his chest, shook his head. "They're just words. They're not real. They're as much a fairy tale as that legend is."

Shock rippled through her at that. She could understand that he didn't love her anymore, that she had to regain his trust. But to deny love even existed… "That's awfully cynical."

"It's the truth. Everyone's out for himself, *querida.* That's just the way this world is."

"Even you?"

He let out a bitter laugh. "Yeah, even me. I'm definitely out for myself."

She didn't believe that. He was the most protective, most loyal man she knew. And he'd loved her once, really loved her. She'd felt the depths of his passion—had felt it again last night.

But he didn't believe it. Or he didn't want to admit it. "So what do you believe in?" she asked.

"Justice." His eyes drilled into hers. "And I'm going to get it."

"But…what if you can't?"

"I will." The deadly conviction in his voice made her breath catch. Failure wasn't an option for this man.

He turned away, stared out the window, and for a long moment, he didn't speak. She studied the implacable planes of his profile, the resolute set of his jaw.

Then the bells in the plaza tolled the quarter hour, and he glanced at her again. "I told you I grew up in the slums."

"El Salobral."

He nodded, frowned. "It's funny. Most people think that when you're poor like that, money's what matters most. But they're wrong. It's not money—it's honor, pride. When you've got nothing, when there's nothing else left, that's the only thing that counts.

"The hunger, you deal with that. It's just normal after a while, the way you feel. But losing your pride…" He shook his head. "I'd rather die as a thief than have to beg."

Her heart rolled. "So that's why you stole? For food?"

"Not for myself so much. I got food in school. I did it for my mom. My old man drank, spent any money we scraped together on booze. And it killed me to watch her beg."

"But I thought…I always heard that Gypsies stuck together, helped each other out."

"Some tried, like my aunt Carmen. She was my mother's sister. But everyone was poor. There wasn't much to go around. And my old man got mean when he drank. People tended to leave us alone."

She nodded, rubbed her arms. "One of my foster fathers drank. I learned to stay away."

"My old man usually disappeared when he drank, got in fights in the bars. But that last time, he came back. He'd gotten it into his head that my mother had been unfaithful." He made a sound of disgust. "She barely had the strength to beg, let alone have an affair. But she couldn't reason with him. She tried."

"You're not saying he killed her?" She tried to keep the horror from her voice.

"Not outright. She died later, from injuries to the brain. The police got to him before my uncles did, so he got sent to jail. That's where he died. I figure my uncles got someone to kill him there." His gaze met hers, and the coldness in his eyes made her heart chill. "Gypsies have ways of exacting justice."

She heard the steel in his voice, thought of his determination to bring down don Fernando and shivered hard. "Is that when your aunt took you in?"

"No." He shot her a sardonic smile. "There was a priest who worked in the slums back then. He'd taken an interest in me, encouraged me to stay in school. He said my family didn't want me, that my aunt wouldn't take me in."

"What? I can't believe that." She'd seen the love in the woman's eyes, the loyalty she felt toward Luke.

"She told me later that she'd looked for me, but she didn't know where I'd gone. And she was afraid to go to the police." He lifted his shoulder. "I don't know. Maybe it's true. But I didn't know that then."

"But…that's horrible." She stared at him, stunned by the cruelty, the hurt inflicted on an innocent child. "And he was a priest? How could he have lied like that?"

"He probably thought he was doing me a favor. Maybe he was. If I'd stayed in El Salobral, I wouldn't have made it much past sixth grade."

"But still…"

"Yeah. Learning your family doesn't want you doesn't help your pride." His eyes held hers. "But I guess you know that."

"Yes." She knew exactly how a rejection like that felt. "So where did you go?"

"To an orphanage, *una casa de acogida*. It had about thirty kids."

She pressed her lips together, tightened her hands on the afghan. "I was in a group home once. I hated it." A bully had made her life miserable.

The corner of his mouth curved up. "It was probably worse for you, *querida*. You're too gentle for that kind of life."

"I'm not weak."

"I didn't say you were weak. Just gentle. There's a difference."

"Is there?"

"Yeah." He moved closer, cupped her chin in his hand. Heat flared in his eyes, and her breath caught.

"You're gentle, elegant, brave. And soft. I like how soft you are." His voice grew deeper, rough. He slipped his free hand under the afghan, touched her bare waist, sending ripples of excitement shimmering through her. His hand slid up her ribs, palmed her breast. And she was lost in his eyes, the thrill of his hands, his heat.

She gasped, swayed toward him, shocked that her body was already softening, turning moist. Just one touch and she ached for him again—urgently, everywhere. Right now.

He stilled, hissed. "Damn. It doesn't go away." And then he lowered his head, fused his mouth to hers and pulled her against his erection. She trembled, his rough jeans incredibly erotic against her bare skin.

But then he groaned, set her away. "You'd better get dressed, or we'll never make it out of here today. You're too tempting."

Tempting was right. The man had the most amazing effect on her—instant, explosive. And she doubted that putting her clothes on would change that.

But she picked up the afghan, walked back to her clothes. And she remembered how he'd taken down that guard in Ávila, how lethal he'd been in that fight. "I take it you fought a lot at the orphanage?"

"I was the only Gypsy there. That made me different. And I was really into picking locks by then, which didn't help. It fed into that whole Gypsy-thief stereotype. So any time anything went missing—food, money, clothes—I got blamed. My enemies started setting me up."

She thought about that as she pulled on her shirt, her jeans. So he'd used his talents just as she had, as a way to escape the loneliness, the pain. But while her talents had gained her acceptance, his had isolated him more.

She slipped on her shoes, glanced back. "Is that why you got arrested?"

"No, I was stupid." He strode over, tugged on his shirt. "I was sixteen and running on hormones. I had a rival at school, a rich *payo* who picked on the other kids. We liked the same girl. I was so hot for her, I didn't know she was playing me, using me to make him jealous. I was dumb enough to think she really liked me."

She tried to imagine him at sixteen—lanky, tough, with that dangerous smile in his eyes. No doubt the girls crowded around him. "What makes you think she didn't?"

"She told me to meet her one night at a house in her neighborhood. The people were on vacation. I went there expecting sex." He let out a bitter laugh. "But her boyfriend set me up. He made it look like I'd robbed the place—along with some others nearby. I never had a chance."

Her heart stumbled as that sank in. "Maybe she wasn't in on it. Maybe the boyfriend did it on his own."

"Well, she sure as hell didn't defend me." His eyes held hers. And she knew what he was thinking. That she had abandoned him, too.

"Luke…" Nerves swarmed through her chest, a sudden panic that jittered her heart. "Oh, God, Luke. I'm so sorry."

She pressed her hand to her throat, swamped by guilt, remorse. She'd done this to him. She'd been the final blow, the one who'd taken him over the edge.

She saw him so clearly now—his battle for dignity, honor, the way everyone had rejected him, blamed him for things that were never his fault.

And he'd stoically picked himself up each time, shouldered the accusations, protected those weaker than him. But with each new wound he'd buried his own feelings deeper, piece by piece, until she'd demolished what was left of his heart.

Until all he had left was his pride.

And don Fernando wanted to rob him of even that.

He moved close, tipped up her chin, and a thick ache blocked off her throat. "I'll keep you safe, *querida*. I promise you that. I'll get you out of this mess alive. But that's all I can give you. I'm not capable of anything else."

Her heart wrenched at the darkness in his voice, the isolation haunting his eyes. He was wrong, so wrong. But he would never believe her words now.

She had to prove it to him, prove that love existed, that he could count on her, that for once, he wasn't alone.

He stepped back, putting distance between them, then reached for his socks and shoes. And she straightened the cushions on the couch, picked up the calendar she'd dropped on the floor, tried not to dwell on the anguish ravaging her gut.

She'd hurt this man deeply, unfairly, and she had to fix that now. She had to figure out where that necklace was, restore his name....

She tossed the calendar on the nearby table, glanced at the photo on the cover, the full moon rising over the Roman Bridge. She paused, frowned, picked up the calendar again.

The full moon. The professor said that society held its ceremonies when the moon was full. And Antonio had kept a calendar with lunar phases on it in his otherwise bare apartment.

She flipped through the pages to the current month, skimmed the dates. Then her heart dipped. The next full moon was tonight.

She swallowed, and a terrible sense of urgency gripped her. She didn't know what the society planned to do with the necklace, but they had to find it fast. But where would they hold their ceremonies? Where had don Fernando gone?

She flipped the page to the previous month, then to the one before that. He traveled so much, it was hard to tell. He lectured, went to auctions. And there'd been that symposium in Paris he couldn't attend because—

Her breath caught. Excitement bubbled up. "Luke." She whirled around, and his eyes met hers. "I know where the necklace is. Don Fernando's *pazo,* his country home in Galicia." A fourteenth-century castle his family had owned since medieval times. "He goes there every few months. And the last time he went, the moon was full."

"Do you know where it is?"

"I think so. It's near Arzúa. I was there once, a few years ago."

He frowned, stood. "That's a six-hour drive, maybe more if we have to take the side roads."

"So we'll need our car."

He shook his head. "It's probably been towed by now. We'll have to find another one."

"I guess." She hated to commit another crime, but they hardly had a choice. They couldn't risk taking a bus.

A sudden pounding caught her attention, the sound of hammering on a nearby door. Her gaze flew to Luke's. "Is it—?"

"Shh." He stepped back, crept to the door.

She wheeled around, her heart pumping fast now, and tossed the afghan over the sofa, fluffed up the pillows, tried to erase any signs that they'd been inside.

Luke strode back to her, snapped off the light. "They're checking the apartments. We need to find another way out."

"Right." But how? The front balcony was out. Police were all over the plaza. And they were only on the first floor here; they didn't have access to the roof.

She turned, rushed into the bedroom. They were in a corner apartment, so the side wall formed part of the deep, arched entrance into the plaza. She pushed the blinds on the side balcony window aside and looked out. A tall, paneled truck was parked just beneath them, probably supplying the bar below.

"Luke, over here. Maybe we can hide inside that truck."

He stalked over, inched open the balcony window. Male voices and the clank of dishes floated up in the cool, morning air. "Not in it," he decided. "On top. On the roof rack. They'll be searching vehicles at the roadblocks.

"You climb down first," he continued. "When you get on the truck, lie down flat, and hold on to the rack. I'll climb down after you."

She nodded, but her nerves fluttered hard. Could they really ride on top of the truck? What if the police saw them there?

Luke held her arm, both of them watching as the driver pulled crates of wine from the back of the truck, loaded them on his dolly.

Then a knock sounded behind them on the apartment door, and she snapped her gaze to Luke's. The police were here. Her nerves fluttered hard. If that truck driver didn't hurry…

Luke's fingers tightened, forcing her to wait. Her heart hammered against her rib cage. She gnawed at her bottom lip. The driver stacked another box on the dolly, finally wheeled it into the bar.

"Okay, go," Luke urged, and she stepped out.

The arches partially hid her on the balcony, but she knew she'd be visible once she dropped to the truck. She swung her injured leg over the wrought-iron railing, then the other, and balanced on the edge. The drop to the truck looked farther than she'd thought, at least five feet.

But she had no choice. She leaped, hit the top of the truck, bit down on her lip to stifle her cry. The truck rocked at the impact, knocking her to her knees. She ignored the pain and lay flat.

Then she inched up her head to watch Luke. He closed the balcony doors behind him, swung his leg over the railing. But then the truck driver came back out. Whistling, the man loaded the dolly into the back of the truck and slammed the rear doors shut.

The whistling stopped abruptly, and she froze. Had he spotted her? Spotted Luke? But she caught a whiff of cigarette smoke, exhaled in relief.

But why didn't he hurry? She could see the tension on Luke's face, the anxiety in his stance. The police had to be in the apartment now. And yet, Luke still couldn't get on the truck.

The driver finally climbed into the cab, started the truck. Luke climbed over the balcony and crouched, ready to jump.

But then the truck lurched, pulled away, and her heart jerked into her throat. Hurry, she silently urged Luke. *Hurry.*

The truck moved again, and he leaped.

And missed.

Chapter 14

Pain tore through Luke's shoulder as he clung to the roof rack, searing his arm like an open flame. The savage burn jolted him, wrenching the breath from his lungs, but he tightened his grip and held on.

He clenched his teeth, grunted, got his foot on the moving truck's bumper, struggled to hoist himself up. Spasms sizzled his shoulder, ripped through his nerves, and he groaned at the sharp stabs of pain.

The truck swayed, hit a bump. He swung out, smashed back, caught hold of the rack with his other hand. Then he forced himself upward, his arm muscles screaming. Sofia helped pull him the rest of the way up.

He collapsed next to her, facedown on the rack. The truck picked up speed, shuddering over the cobblestones, and he hissed out an agonized breath.

What had he done to his arm?

He forced his head up, slid his glance to Sofia, made sure she was lying flat, safe. Sweat popped out on his forehead, the edges of his vision blurred, and he dropped his head down again.

He couldn't pass out. Not now. The police could still see them, discover them at a roadblock. He had to protect Sofia, keep her safe...

"Luke, are you all right?" Her voice sounded faint, as if she were fading away.

He blinked, struggled to stay conscious. "I'm fine," he gritted out, and then the world turned black.

The whine of the gears shifting down, the wild jolt as the engine changed speeds jerked Luke awake. He lay prone on the vibrating truck, his cheek pressed against the metal roof rack.

Sofia shifted beside him, and he lifted his head, but a fierce spasm seized his shoulder and mauled him with pain. He lowered his head, fought back nausea, groaned.

He didn't have time for this now.

He forced his eyes open again, slid his gaze to the sky. The round moon was fading near the horizon, the sun still rising beyond the hills. Early morning. So he hadn't been out for long.

The truck slowed even more, rumbled past the low stone buildings of a dusty *pueblo,* then wheezed to a stop beside a bar. The driver climbed out, banged the cab door shut, and went inside. Luke let out a strangled groan.

"Luke." Sofia sat up, touched his shoulder, and he flinched. "Are you all right?"

"Yeah." Using his good arm, he pushed himself to a sitting position, shook off the dizziness that bludgeoned his head. "We need to get off this truck."

"Wait, I'll help."

She slid down first, then braced him as he inched off the end. Her weight blocked his fall, kept him from pitching head first in the dirt.

Swearing at how weak he felt, he stumbled around the bar toward a shed. He made it as far as a plastic crate propped against the wall, collapsed onto it, wheezed in a breath.

"What happened to your arm?" Sofia crouched next to him, gently probed his shoulder, and he nearly went under again. "Do you think it's broken?"

"No." He wouldn't let it be. "It's just a strain."

"Can you move it?"

"Yeah." He tried to straighten his arm to the side, but even that small movement made him sweat. But he couldn't worry about his injured arm now. "Where are we?"

"Just outside of Zamora."

He started to nod, thought better of it. They were an hour north of Salamanca, past the roadblocks at least. But they still had five hours to go—more if they had to avoid the main roads.

He stood, tried not to sway. "We'd better find a car."

"I'll look. You stay here and rest."

"I'll rest in the car." He shook off the dizziness, pushed the pain from his mind, strode down the narrow dirt road.

She caught up with him a second later. "You know you're stubborn."

"Yeah." He slid her a grin, let his eyes linger on the gentle swell of her cheeks, the graceful slope of her neck. And a sudden warmth moved into his chest. If stubborn meant protective, then she was right. And he was going to get a lot more protective before this journey ended.

But he wouldn't break that news to her yet.

He spotted a late model Fiat down the road. "Can you drive a stick?"

"Yes."

"Good. You can drive." He glanced at the sky. The moon was barely visible now with the rising sun, but it still looked ominously full. "And Sofia…" His eyes met hers. "Drive fast."

By the time they reached Galicia in the northwest corner of Spain, it was raining. Luke bolted down the last bit of cod empanada they'd picked up at a local *panadería*, frowned out the windshield at the one-lane road. He didn't believe in omens, but the dreary mist hanging over the mountains, the huge, lead-lined clouds looming on the horizon did nothing to settle his nerves. And that tension he'd felt since they'd seen that professor in Salamanca kept getting stronger, tighter, gripping his skull like a piercing claw.

"How's your arm?" Sofia asked from behind the wheel.

"Not bad," he lied. "The ibuprofen helped. Are we getting close?"

"I think so. It should be just ahead."

He grunted, pulled his attention back to the winding road. They drove by farms, stone fences covered in ivy, dairy cows lowing in fields. A woman in typical country clothes—scarf, rubber boots, leggings under her knee-length dress—leaned on her hoe and watched them pass.

The place was peaceful. Too peaceful. Even the relentless tick of the windshield wipers added to his pent-up nerves.

But what else could he do? He had to get that necklace. He didn't know what that society planned to do with it, but lives could be at risk. That professor said they killed Gypsies to prove their loyalty. And there was a full moon tonight.

But he couldn't ignore his instincts. He had to be careful, keep Sofia safe. So he would enter that castle alone.

Now he had to convince her of that.

"There it is." She slowed the car, pointed at a crumbling stone tower barely visible through the leafy trees. He leaned forward, but couldn't see much.

"Drive past it," he said. "We'll hide the car and walk back."

By the time they left the car on a tractor path, shielded from the road by a cluster of trees, the rain had lightened to a chilly drizzle. Luke trailed Sofia up the road to the castle, taking in the low stone walls bordering the fields, the clank of cowbells, the sound of a river rushing through a hidden gorge.

And he had to admit it was a good spot for secret activities. Aside from the occasional shepherd or farmer, they hadn't seen a person in hours.

They stopped within sight of the castle, ducked behind a thicket of trees. The keep jutted into the leaden sky, its ancient stones stained orange with moss. Four smaller, rectangular towers with crossbow slits fortified the crumbling stone wall.

If there'd ever been a drawbridge, it was gone. Instead, an elevated grass track with a dozen cars parked beside it led to the wooden door. A lone guard with the ruddy complexion of a local man stood watch.

Suddenly, Sofia grabbed his good arm. "There's don Fernando's car."

Luke switched his gaze to the cars. "Recognize any of the others?"

She studied the cars, shook her head.

"Come on." He motioned for her to follow, led the way through the woods to the back. They skirted the field below the castle, studied the layout, paused to examine the curtain wall that ringed the fortified complex.

But while the castle was crumbling in spots, it still did what it was designed to do—it kept intruders out. And even if he managed to find a weak spot in the wall, he'd never be able to scale it with his injured arm.

Sofia shivered beside him, and he glanced down. "Are you cold?"

"A little. It's just…" She paused, and he saw the anxiety lurking in her eyes. "I have a terrible feeling about this."

So did he. There were too many unknowns, too much that could go wrong. He hadn't installed the security on this place, didn't know what was inside.

And the place was eerily silent. There was no movement, no signs of activity, only one guard.

And it unnerved him.

"Come on. Let's go back to the car."

They completed the circle, crept back to the car and slid inside. "So what do you think?" Sofia asked, her eyes still worried.

He thought they should get away fast. But he had to get that necklace first. "We'll have to go through the front door."

"How? We can't just walk in."

"No. We'll have to create a distraction. When it's dark enough, I'll hide in the bushes by the entrance. I want you to drive up in the car and block the road. When the guard walks over to see what's wrong, I'll go inside. Then you drive away. But be sure to get out of there before he sees your face."

She frowned. "But how will I get in?"

He inhaled, knowing she wasn't going to like this part. "You won't. You'll drive the car back here and wait for me."

Her mouth sagged, and then she snapped it shut. "Try again."

"Sofia—"

"No, absolutely not. No! You can't go in there alone. It's too dangerous. What if Paco sees you? What if he tries to kill you?"

"It'll be more dangerous if we're both in there." He

exhaled. "Look, I'll be fine. I'll slip in, then out, just grab the necklace and run."

"Then I'll slip in and out of there with you." She folded her arms, her face set in stubborn lines.

"Forget it. One of us has to stay outside."

"Then I'll go in."

"The hell you will." Outrage deadened his voice. "You'll stay in the car and distract the guard. And if anything goes wrong—and it won't," he added when she inhaled, "call my cousin Manolo in Madrid." He rummaged in the glove compartment with his good hand, scrawled the number down. "He'll know what to do." He'd get her someplace safe.

"But Luke—"

"For God's sake, Sofia, please." He touched her face, locked his eyes on hers, his fear for her churning his gut. "Do this for me. Promise me you'll stay in the car."

Her frown deepened. "But—"

"Please. Promise me." He lifted her chin, swamped by the need to keep her safe. Because if anything happened to her… He swallowed hard, fought back the dread. "I'll work better if I know you're safe."

A furrow creased her brows, and he thought she'd argue more. But then she exhaled, and the soft sound eased his heart. "All right. But if you're not back—"

"I will be." He drew her face closer, stroked his thumb along her jaw, breathed in the heat of her skin. His gaze dropped to her lips, the swell of her breasts.

And that familiar hunger surged through him, the need to protect her, possess her, surround himself with her heat.

"Luke." Her voice was breathless, soft. "Your arm—"

He kissed her, silencing her, letting his body speak for his heart. And she shuddered against him, blasting away everything except the delirious feel of her in his arms.

* * *

The moon rose over the castle that night, full and pale and stark. The wind had come up, chasing clouds across its face, and rustling the bushes where Luke crouched. He waited, watched the guard slouch against the door, felt the damp chill rise through his shoes.

But that discomfort was nothing compared to his fear for Sofia, the foreboding thrumming his nerves. He'd spent the past hours turning over his plan in his mind, examining it from every angle, trying to anticipate what could go wrong. He had the gun and knife from the guard in Ávila. He'd given Sofia his cousin Manolo's phone number, shown her how to hot-wire the car. And she'd described everything she knew about the castle to him, although, truthfully, it wasn't much.

All he could do now was wait.

But he couldn't quell the knot in his gut, the anxiety prickling his skin. The worry that she was in danger, that he'd be unable to keep her safe.

Then the sound of the car's engine rose on the wind, and the headlights cut through the night. He tensed, kept his eye on the guard stirring to life. The car turned into the private lane, headed toward them, and the guard stepped forward to see.

As planned, Sofia drove closer until she'd nearly reached the door. Then she stopped, started to turn around, drove forward, back, idled, blocking the narrow lane.

And then the car died.

Luke's heart skipped, beat hard. She'd stalled—not part of the plan. But he'd shown her how to hot-wire the car; she could manage without the key.

He hoped.

He waited, his pulse picking up speed, but she didn't

restart the car. What was she doing? Why was she taking so long? She couldn't risk being seen.

The guard left his post, headed toward the car.

Not happy with the situation, but knowing he had to go in, Luke crept from the bushes, moved to the castle door.

But then Sofia popped the car's hood open and climbed out. He froze, his hand on the castle door. Why was she getting out of the car?

The guard approached her, and she ducked under the hood. Luke opened the door to the castle, hesitated again.

Damn, he didn't like this. This was his one chance to get inside. But how could he leave Sofia? He was counting on her to stay safe.

"*¿Qué pasa?*" he heard the guard ask.

"*No sé.*" Sofia murmured back.

The guard peered under the hood. Seconds passed. And then suddenly, as if suspicious, the guard glanced his way.

Oh, hell.

The guard straightened. "*¡Oye!*" He reached for his gun. "*¿Qué haces allí?*"

But Sofia grabbed the hood and slammed it down, and the edge glanced off the man's head. He fell, sprawled on the ground and didn't move.

Luke blinked. His admiration surged.

He ran to Sofia, grabbed the guard's foot, ignored the sharp pain stabbing his arm. "What happened?"

"I couldn't see the wires, and I was afraid to turn on the light." She took the other leg and helped drag the guard into the trees. "Is he… Do you think he's dead?"

"No, just stunned." He knelt, handed her the man's radio and gun. "That was good thinking on your part."

He rose and kissed her hard. "I'll start the car. Then get the hell out of here."

He slid into the car, started the engine, crawled back out. "Okay, go. I won't be long."

"Luke…" She clutched his sleeve, and her voice wobbled. "Be careful."

"Yeah." He'd be careful, all right. Foreboding screamed through his skull.

He raced back to the castle door, cracked it open, glanced back as she drove away. At least she'd be safe now. He sucked in his breath and walked in.

"Bienvenido." Welcome.

Luke froze. The familiar voice crawled through his nerves. Don Fernando stepped out of the darkness, his pistol trained on Luke's chest.

"Luke Moreno. I thought you'd make it. We have business to finish, no?"

"Yeah." They had unfinished business, all right. Five years of unfinished business.

Luke met his eyes, his deadly, bitter eyes. The eyes of the man who'd hated him, framed him. The man who'd used his power and wealth to destroy him.

The eyes of the man who wanted Sofia dead.

Luke's face burned as his anger rose, and he shook with the need to attack. Even though the man was armed, he knew he could bring him down.

But then a dozen thugs slipped from the shadows, and his heart went still.

"Your gun," don Fernando ordered. "Throw it down."

Luke tugged the pistol from his waistband, tossed it down, his gaze locked on those ruthless eyes. And a chill crept through him, a raw fear that congealed in his gut. Sofia was out there alone.

And don Fernando knew it.

The man jerked his head, motioning to someone behind him. Luke turned, but his skull exploded in pain.

He slumped down, his vision dimming.

And prayed that Sofia stayed safe.

Chapter 15

Someone was out there.

Sofia huddled in the car in the darkness, the cold air chilling her skin. The wind moaned in the pines overhead. An owl hooted, then hooted again. Fear crept along her spine, slid into her throat.

Someone was out there, watching her, hunting her.

Hardly breathing, she waited, tried to shake off the burgeoning dread. But she could feel him getting closer, closer.

She sucked in a breath, rubbed her arms, tried to reason away the fear. She was just worried about Luke. He should have been back by now. But not that much time had passed since he'd gone in, had it? How would she know? Every second he was away felt like a year.

She bent forward, fingered the wires beneath the dash, tempted to start the car to see the clock. But then she paused. No, if someone was out there, she didn't dare tip him off.

Oh, God. Was someone really out there?

She held her breath, listened, but her pulse thundered inside her skull. She snapped off the interior light, picked up the guard's gun from the passenger seat, then slowly lifted the latch on the door. She inched it open and listened again.

It had grown quiet in the woods. Too quiet.

Panic screamed through her nerves.

Breathe, she reminded herself wildly. Stay calm. Calm! She forced herself to move, to step carefully out of the car.

The full moon lit the narrow road—dim, but enough to expose her to searching eyes. But if she escaped through the woods she would make too much noise.

She adjusted the gun in her trembling hand, choked back the hysteria swarming her throat. And a vision flashed into her mind—Antonio's splattered skull and vacant eyes.

A twig snapped.

She ran.

She bolted up the road, panicked, her breath sawing fast, fast, fast. She ran harder, delirious with fear, the frantic need to escape lashing her brain. She had to get off the road, find a gap in the wall, an opening she could cut through.

Forget it. She scrambled over the low stone wall, skinning her palms, bumping her leg, then crashed through a stand of wet shrubs.

Run. Run!

She dodged into the woods, plowed through the undergrowth, twisted through thick vines and shrubs. She stumbled, tripped over a log, and sprawled face first into wet ferns. Terrified, she leaped to her feet and rushed on.

Her lungs burned. Her vision blurred. Panic hammered her mind. And then she saw the castle, where Luke was. *Luke.* She slowed, stopped behind a tree, and gasped for breath.

For a minute, she couldn't think. She braced her hand on

the bark, pulled air through her fiery lungs, tried to settle her rioting pulse. Think. She had to think. She shuddered, forced in more air, lifted her head.

A cluster of men stood by the cars now. She could see them laughing, talking in the eerie moonlight, but their voices were too low to catch.

She had to get closer, to learn what they were saying, find out what had happened to Luke. She glanced around, listened, her heart rapping hard in her chest. Was her pursuer still out there? Had he followed her here?

She couldn't think about that. She had to find Luke, make sure he was safe.

Struggling to beat back the terror and the instincts screaming at her to flee, she crept through the bushes toward the men. She positioned herself as close as she dared, strained to hear around the pulse pounding her ears, while urgency flayed at her nerves.

She caught phrases, words—a jumble of Portuguese, Castellano, Gallego—and then her heart thudded into her throat. They'd captured a man, a Gypsy. They'd knocked him out, locked him up.

Luke. She clamped her hand on her mouth, muffled a cry.

They kill a Gypsy, the professor had said. Fear gripped her gut, a stark icy terror that chilled straight through her bones. She had to get him out of there fast.

But how?

Frantic, her stomach roiling with panic and despair, she tried to think what to do. Go in alone? No, even with the gun she had, she could hardly battle the guards. But she couldn't trust the police to help—she'd learned that lesson in Salamanca. Plus, who would believe her? Don Fernando had connections, power. His family had owned land here for six hundred years. And she didn't even have proof of a crime.

She rubbed her forehead with trembling hands, tried to beat back the panic and fear. She had to think up a plan. It was up to her to save Luke.

She glanced at the moon looming over the castle, the frozen shriek on its face echoing her fear.

And knew that whatever she did, she had to do it fast.

Pain. It burned down his shoulder, shot through his arm, throbbed through his battered skull. Luke cracked open one eye, tried to lift his face from the dirt, but a spasm tore through his nerves. He slumped back down and sucked in his breath.

He lay facedown on a damp dirt floor. His ankles were bound, his arms wrenched brutally behind his back. The air was dank, musty, dark.

He shifted, groaned at the agonizing bolt of pain, determined not to throw up. He closed his eyes again, panted, waited until the nausea had passed, choked back the bile in his throat.

All right. All right. He wasn't going to pass out again. He was going to get to his feet, get free, find Sofia.

Panic surged at the thought of Sofia, but he forced the fear from his mind. He had to think, get himself out of this mess, then worry about protecting her.

Bracing himself for the pain this time, he rolled onto his shoulder and hissed. Sweat beaded his face. Shivers shuddered along his spine, but he kept working his way to his knees.

He made it. He sagged back on his heels, dragged in his breath, blinked back the dizziness making his head weave. A knot pulsed on his scalp. Blood dripped down his jaw. His arms and legs were numb.

He tugged his wrists, tested the cord. Too tight. He leaned back, felt along his calves, searched again. But the guards had been thorough. They'd taken both the gun and the knife.

Now what?

He blew out his breath, searched the gloom. He was in a wine cellar, a *bodega,* with a dirt floor and rough stone walls. The only light came from a small iron grate high on the opposite wall—too small for him to climb through. Stone stairs led to the only door—which would be guarded, no doubt.

So there was no way out. But they couldn't leave him here forever. And he had to be ready when they came. Balancing carefully, he leaned forward, rocked back, tipped forward again, then heaved himself to his feet.

He swayed, breathed deeply, waited for the spinning to pass. Then he inched his way around the room, hunting for something to saw off his binds. Because he knew one thing. He was getting out of this hole.

And when he did, don Fernando had better watch out.

Climb, run, limp, listen. Climb, run, limp, listen.

Sofia kept as close to the road as she dared, scooting from tree to tree, darting across open pastures in the moonlight, skirting rocks, and scaling hills.

The elderly farm couple who'd answered their door had thought she was part of the *Santa Compaña,* a ghost. She supposed she looked like one by now—muddy, wet, hysterical, her hair wild and clothes torn. But at least they'd let her use their phone.

She'd decided that her only hope of saving Luke lay in numbers. She didn't know who to trust, which police were honest, which ones corrupt. But if she could get enough witnesses here, enough people to see what was going on—newscasters, farmers, police—don Fernando wouldn't be able to hide the truth. And even his influence couldn't override the testimony of dozens of bystanders. So she'd phoned the local and federal police, asked the elderly couple to mobilize neighbors, begged Luke's cousin to contact every media outlet in Spain.

And now she was heading back to the castle again. But she couldn't let don Fernando's men see her yet. She had to enter from the other direction, make it seem as if she'd come from the car. Because if she hoped to make this plan work—if she hoped to keep Luke alive until help arrived—she had to appear to be acting alone.

She paused, pressed her hand to her belly to still her nerves. It was a terrible risk. Don Fernando would capture and disarm her the minute she neared the castle, she knew that. And if he didn't believe her, both she and Luke would be dead.

She hauled in a shaky breath, and doubts piled up in her mind. Could she really pull this off, make it work? Could she convince don Fernando that she was on his side?

And what if help didn't get here in time? What if don Fernando didn't believe her? Even worse—what if Luke did?

She waffled, the fear of failure warring with the dread of success. She'd be playing on Luke's bitter past, striking at his most vulnerable point. And if he didn't trust her...

She swallowed. She had no choice. She had to do this. It was Luke's only hope.

She straightened, prayed for courage, climbed to the lane that led to the castle's door.

And prepared to betray the man she loved.

In the movies, cutting a rope with a broken bottle was simple, fast. In reality, it took an eternity, or at least long enough for Luke's panic to build, for his worry over Sofia to swell into churning fear.

Because if don Fernando hurt her...

An image of Sofia flashed into his mind—her gentle

smile, her soft, lush curves. He closed his eyes, weak with
the need to hold her, protect her, hear the sweet, lilting sound
of her voice.

The glass slid from his blood-soaked hands, fell to the dirt.
He searched for it in the dark with his foot, then began the
slow, painful process of picking it up.

He couldn't let himself worry about Sofia. He had to concentrate, focus on cutting these ropes so he could get himself
out of this pit.

But then her voice slipped into his mind again, and he
shook his head. He must be losing it, getting delirious if he
was starting to hear her voice. That blow to the skull had done
more damage than he'd thought.

He squatted, grappled for the shard of glass on the floor,
ignored the twinge as it sliced through his palm. But her
voice floated on the cool night air again, louder this time, and
he grew still.

He wasn't imagining it. She was here, in the castle.

Fear crawled through his gut, seeped into his bones. Why
hadn't she listened to him? Why hadn't she called Manolo?
Why hadn't she driven away?

His mind flashed to his aunt, her body bloody, splattered with
gore, and panic shot through his nerves. He had to get Sofia out
of here. They'd torture her, kill her. She didn't stand a chance.

Desperate now, he wrapped the slippery glass in his blood-
soaked shirt, sawed viciously at the cords. He worked the
shard back and forth, ignoring the blood, the pain.

The cord frayed, loosened, snapped apart. He jerked his
arms forward, groaned as his circulation returned with prickling stabs, then the savage burn in his arm. He sucked in air,
wiped his trembling hands on his shirt, waited for the agony
to subside. Then he picked up the broken glass with his good
hand, got to work on his feet. Long seconds later, he was free.

He leaped up, nearly fell. He shook his legs, waited impatiently for the numbness to pass, then limped to the high, narrow grille.

Sofia's voice was louder, closer now, but he couldn't see out the grate. He dragged a barrel to the wall, climbed up, and peered into the courtyard's gloom. A cluster of men stood in the rubble near the central keep, the same guards who had overpowered him. But there was a strange intensity about them now, an undercurrent pulsing the air.

Then a man moved aside, and Luke's heart began to thud. Sofia stood proud and defiant before the group of men, her dark hair wild, her hands tied behind her back. Her wet clothes molded her curves.

And he knew what those men were thinking. What any man would think. That she was female, ripe, helpless. And he knew with a chilling certainty the danger she was in.

She lifted her chin, exposing the feminine line of her throat, said something he couldn't make out. He pulled in his breath, tried to calm the blood rocketing through his ears, the need to charge over and hide her from view.

"…to you alone."

Don Fernando stepped forward and answered something Luke couldn't catch.

"Hardly," she scoffed. "Tied up like this?"

Luke tightened his jaw, knowing every man out there was eyeing her breasts, calculating his odds. And if that bastard let anyone touch her…

Don Fernando signaled to the guards to leave, but they just muttered and didn't move. *"Ahora,"* he barked, and they drifted off.

Luke slowly inched out his breath. Don Fernando still had control of his men. But for how long?

Don Fernando motioned toward a stone bench built into the

wall, just feet from where Luke crouched. Sofia limped toward it, perched awkwardly on the edge. So close he could see the anxiety in her eyes, the effort it had cost to face those men.

"You didn't have to tie me up," she said to don Fernando, sounding hurt. "I only wanted to talk." Her patron didn't answer, and she shook her head. "I just…I don't understand. What happened? I trusted you. I worked with you. And I thought you cared about me."

Don Fernando lowered himself beside her, heaved out a sigh. "I didn't want it to come to this, believe me. I tried to protect you, to keep you out. But now…" He spread his hands.

"But why didn't you tell me what you were doing? If you'd told me you were looking for the treasures, I could have helped."

"I couldn't do that." He sounded shocked.

"Why not? I wouldn't have told anyone."

"You don't understand. We're sworn to secrecy. I'd be killed if I broke my pledge."

"But I thought… Aren't you in charge?"

He looked at her. "The professor didn't tell you?"

"Tell me what?"

Don Fernando rose, paced away, turned back. The low lights surrounding the keep cast shadows on his face, making his high-bred features harsh. "When we become soldiers, we swear obedience to the king."

The king? Luke blinked. The society still had a king? There was someone even more powerful out there?

Don Fernando's voice dropped, and Luke craned forward to hear. "His power reaches everywhere, around the world. And I could never betray him. My ancestors have been Black Crescent knights for a thousand years."

"But…" She sounded as confused as Luke felt. "Is that

why you're interested in antiquities? Because of the Roma treasures?"

"They're not Roma." Don Fernando whirled back to her, his voice so vicious that Luke's pulse jerked. "The Gypsies stole those treasures. They belong to the king!"

Sofia cringed, shrank back on the bench. "Sorry. I...I didn't know."

Don Fernando resumed pacing, and Luke hissed out his breath. This man was on edge, dangerous. She needed to be careful not to provoke him.

Don Fernando turned again, shrugged. "I knew they wouldn't show up on the legal market, but I wasn't worried about that. I have contacts in the black market, too. But I needed someone who understood the stones, who could feel their power. Someone who could tell the real treasures from the fakes. And when I saw your work, I knew you were the one."

Sofia gaped at him. "You mean...the scholarship, the internship—that was all because of the legend?"

"I couldn't do it alone," he explained. "And you were perfect. You had the talent, the gift. You could even replicate the pieces if I needed it done. And you needed me. At least until that *gitano* came along."

"So you framed Luke." Her voice went flat.

"I couldn't risk losing you. You were crazy about him. Everyone could see it. I was worried that you'd quit, that he'd take you away."

Luke blinked. So that was why the man despised him. Not only was he a Gypsy, but he'd threatened his hold over Sofia. So don Fernando had played her perfectly, preyed on her insecurities, her need for acceptance, made her believe Luke had used her to get those gems.

The wind picked up, moaned through the gaps in the crumbling wall. "I loved him, you know," she said softly, and

Luke's heart stilled. "But that's…over now. He doesn't love me anymore. He even said so. And I…well, that's in the past." She shook her head, rose. "And I've got an offer to make."

Luke's head came up, and a sudden fear crept into his gut. What was she planning? These men were ruthless. They'd already killed Antonio—their own partner. And they would see through any ruse.

"It won't do any good," don Fernando said, sounding apologetic. "I've already told you. What happens to you now is out of my hands."

"Even if I know where the other treasures are?"

Don Fernando stopped, pivoted slowly toward her.

"I might not have been looking for them," she said. "But I've seen things over the years, heard things, when I was in the Baltic region, with Luke… I just didn't put it together until now."

"And now you want to find them?"

"No, not really. I mean, I'd like to see them. The gems must be amazing. You know how much I love amber. But that's not what I'm really after."

Don Fernando watched her, his eyes narrowed now, alert. "Then what do you want?"

"I want my life back." She moved closer, stood before her patron and lifted her chin. "I'll find the treasures for you. I don't care what you do with them. That's your business. But I want my name cleared, my reputation restored so I can continue my work."

A sliver of doubt snaked into Luke's gut. Of course she wasn't really bargaining for her job. This had to be a ploy— a dangerous one. Because this man would never honor any agreement he made.

"And why should I believe you?" don Fernando asked.

"I've never lied to you. I've always helped you, been on your side."

"You ran off with Luke."

"He forced me to. He made me show him the safe where the necklace was. And then I got shot. People were trying to kill me. I was terrified. I didn't know who to trust, what to do. And I called you from Madrid, remember? I never tried to hide from you."

Luke stared at her, incredulous, not wanting to believe what he'd heard. She *had* to be lying. Of course she was lying. She couldn't be abandoning him, betraying him. Not after the way she'd made love to him, cared for him. He'd seen the sincerity in her eyes, her devastation over don Fernando's deception. She wasn't that good an actress.

Was she?

Or had she decided to switch sides?

He curled his hands into fists, clamped his jaw, shoved back the onrush of doubts. Of course she wouldn't do that. No way would she betray him again.

The more sincere she seemed, the greater the betrayal.

"I want you to clear my name." Her voice turned fierce now, harder. "I want my work back, my life back. That's all I want. All I've ever wanted. It's the only thing that matters to me."

Luke's pulse stumbled hard. Disbelief mingled with pain. She'd said the same thing to him in that field.

Don Fernando watched her. "And Luke?"

She bit her lip, hesitated. "Do what you have to do. I just...don't want to see it." Her voice wobbled, and she sounded so convincing that his heart plunged. "But I'd like to talk to him first. I think he might know something, from his aunt, I mean. I just need to check out the clues."

Don Fernando still studied her, one wiry brow raised, his skepticism clear.

"You can listen if you want," she said quickly. "I don't care. It's just…with something this important, I'd like to make sure."

A cloud scuttled over the moon. The wind kicked up again, making a lonely moan through the wall. And Luke raged inside, fighting the truth, not wanting to believe what he'd heard. This had to be a trick. She didn't really intend to betray him. She wasn't selling her soul for her career.

He closed his eyes, buffeted by doubts, but her words echoed back, and the truth of them slashed at his pride. She'd told him how much acceptance meant, how much her work mattered to her. But, like a fool, he'd thought he mattered more.

The betrayal knifed deep in his heart.

"I'm sorry," don Fernando said, sounding amazingly sincere. "It's really out of my hands now. The king will be here soon. He'll have to decide." He raised his hand, snapped his fingers, and Paco emerged from the gloom. "Put her in the keep until he arrives."

The bodyguard strode forward and grabbed her arm, but Sofia dug in her heels and turned back.

"Please," she whispered to don Fernando. "I'm telling you the truth. You can trust me on this."

Trust. A crazed laugh bubbled inside him. What the hell did she know about trust?

Loyalty, honor, love—those words meant nothing to her. She was as fake as that necklace she'd made.

His fury swelled. Bitterness raged through his blood. But if she wanted trust, he'd show it to her. Because before this night ended, she could *trust* him to get revenge.

Chapter 16

She was going to die. And with her arms tied, guards everywhere, she couldn't get away.

Trembling, Sofia stumbled beside Paco toward the keep. Feared beat through her skull. Panic reeked from her pores. But she battled back the waves of hysteria, fought to regain control. She had to stay calm, keep her head.

And not make it easy for them.

A guard opened the tower door as they approached. His dark eyes scraped over her, the lewd twist to his lips making her flesh crawl. But she lifted her chin, stared him down until Paco yanked her away.

"Ven conmigo," Paco told the guard, and her heart quaked. Why did Paco want him along?

He dragged her into the musty tower, and the dank air caught in her lungs. She glanced around at the rough stone walls, then jerked her arm from his grasp. He might plan to kill her, but she refused to walk willingly to her death.

He hit her. Fire erupted in her skull, and she cried out, fell to her knees. Dizzy, blinded by pain, she gasped for breath. The men's laughter echoed in her ears.

Paco hauled her upright, yanked her up the stairs, and she struggled to keep her balance. Her head throbbed. Blood mixed with sweat and stung her eyes.

But she refused to cry, refused to let him see her fear.

They passed the first floor, continued up the ancient steps. When they reached the second landing, Paco jerked open the wooden door and shoved her inside.

She stumbled, whirled back, and his cold, flat eyes met hers. His hand went for his gun, and she froze.

She was going to die.

Terror congealed her lungs, streaked down her spine. But she forced her chin up, held his gaze, refusing to cower, to beg. But then he laughed, a high, eerie laugh that made her scalp prick. He stalked out and bolted the door.

She sagged, shuddered, gasped at air. She was alive, alive! At least for now. But her hands were tied. She was locked in the tower, with that disgusting man guarding the door.

She staggered across the empty room and collapsed on a wooden bench. Her arms were numb, her battered cheek throbbed, and she could hardly see from one eye.

And Luke… Where was Luke? Was he injured? Unconscious? Was he even alive?

She closed her eyes, beat back the panic surging inside. What if she'd failed him? What if help didn't get here on time? What if, by letting herself get captured, she'd only made things worse?

She tugged in a breath, opened her eyes. Help would come. Luke's cousin would make sure of that. She was alone in the world, but Luke had family, people who cared. And they'd do everything they could to save his life.

She pressed her trembling lips together, gazed at the full moon gleaming through the crossbow slit in the wall. So where was Luke? Was he watching the moon? Thinking of her?

The wind thrashed the woods around the castle, wailed through the crumbling stone wall. And dread crept through her heart, chilled her to her bones.

Because if she was wrong, by daybreak she and Luke would both be dead.

Let it go. Let it go! Luke fought back the fury flaying his gut, the bitter rage hazing his brain. He couldn't think about Sofia, couldn't let her betrayal distract him from his goal. He had to keep his head, make plans, get out of here alive. He'd deal with her treachery later, once he was free.

He jerked in his breath, forced his mind from Sofia, focused on don Fernando pacing by the keep. The man's head was down, his steps growing more erratic.

Good. A nervous man made mistakes. Luke would be ready when he did.

The door to the keep opened then, and Paco stepped out— alone. Luke's lungs stilled. So the other guard had stayed with Sofia.

He clenched his hands, wanting to charge over there, wrench Sofia from the leering guard. Because no matter what she'd done, he'd promised to protect her. And if that guard touched her...

Let it go, he reminded himself fiercely. He couldn't dwell on her now. He had to form a plan, keep himself under control, find a way out of this mess.

Paco strode over to don Fernando, just several feet from where Luke stood. "She's on the second floor."

Good to know. He'd head there once he escaped this pit.

Don Fernando paced toward the wall, turned back. "I don't like this. I don't trust her."

Paco's expression stayed blank. "What do you want me to do?"

"Get rid of the Gypsy. We can't take a chance that he'll escape. Not with the king flying in tonight."

So they intended to kill him.

"And the body?"

Don Fernando paced again, stopped. "Leave it there. We'll dump it with the others when the ceremony's done."

Others? Luke frowned. So he wasn't the only one being held here. The danger was as bad as he'd thought.

Don Fernando glanced at his watch. "Come get me when you've finished. I'm going to prepare." He turned on his heel, strode into the keep. The bodyguard headed to the bodega door.

Luke's pulse thumped, jolting him into action. He leaped off the barrel, searched for a way to even the odds. His gaze landed on the unlit lightbulb dangling from the ceiling. His eyes were used to the dark. Paco's weren't. But the light switch was outside, beyond his control. He dragged the barrel across the room, climbed up, and removed the bulb.

That done, he scooped up the piece of glass from the dirt, grabbed another bottle of wine. Then he bounded up the stone steps, wedged the bottle under his injured arm, and plastered himself to the wall. He waited, fingered the shard of glass. His pulse rapped fast in his throat.

The bolt on the door scraped back, and the door creaked wide. Paco's silhouette filled the space.

"*Enciende la luz,*" he snapped to someone outside. *Turn on the light.*

"*Ya la encendí,*" a man protested. *I already did.*

So Paco wasn't alone. It would be two against one. Hell of a time to have a bum arm.

Paco swore at the broken light. He moved further into the bodega and went down a step. Luke lobbed the piece of glass across the room, and it landed in the dirt with a thump. Paco whirled toward the sound, and Luke kicked the door shut, crashed the bottle over his head. Paco tottered, reached for his gun. Luke struck him again.

The man fell, didn't move. *One down.* But Luke couldn't take the time to secure him without alerting the guard.

He leaped down the steps, grabbed the bodyguard's gun, dragged him away from the door. Then he ran back up. *"Oye,"* he called to the guard outside. *"Ven aquí.* Help me with this."

The door swung open, and the guard came in. Luke smashed the butt of the pistol against his head and watched him fall. Then he retrieved his gun, tucked it into his waistband, stepped outside and locked the door.

Now to find the prisoners don Fernando had mentioned— as well as the woman who had betrayed him.

His gut churned at the thought of Sofia. Anger mixed with fear for her safety, then settled into grim resolve. No matter what she'd done, she didn't deserve to die. So he would find her, make sure she safely escaped this place—and then get her out of his life.

He blinked the sweat from his eyes, glanced around the courtyard, but the area around the towers were clear. Too clear. Where had everyone gone? Keeping his eye out for patrolling guards, he crept through the shadows toward the keep.

But then a shout rang out, and he ducked behind a rock. Two guards ran past. Then more guards raced through the bailey to a corner tower.

"Viene gente," someone shouted from the wall. *"Desde el bosque."*

People were approaching from the woods? Luke frowned at that odd news. But whoever they were, at least they were distracting the guards. Confident that no one was watching him now, he jogged toward the center keep.

The keep was the tallest structure in the compound, a rectangular tower stretching three stories into the sky. Luke paused outside the entrance, readied his pistol, then charged past the thick, wooden door. Empty.

His pulse thudding hard now, he inched up the spiraling stone steps. When he reached the room off the first floor landing, he shouldered open that door and burst in.

Three people shrank back against the wall. Luke peered at them through the musty gloom, took in their dark hair and skin, the woman's long skirts and braided hair. Roma.

He strode toward them, and the young man rose, his chin raised in defiance, his arms stretched out to protect his daughter and wife. "Are you Calé?" Luke asked in the Gypsy language.

The man studied him for a moment, then lowered his arms. *"Sí."*

"Here. *Toma.*" Luke handed him one of the guns he'd confiscated, tugged the other from the waistband of his jeans. "Are there more people here? More prisoners?"

The man shook his head. "I don't know."

Luke glanced at the woman again. She'd wrapped her arms around her small daughter, was clearly distraught and battling tears. As much as Luke could use the help, she needed her husband more.

"Get your family out," Luke told the man. "I'll check the compound." And rescue Sofia.

His pulse beating hard now, he strode from the room.

Gunshots and shouts came from the courtyard, the sounds muffled by the dense stone walls. He crept up the curving steps to the second floor—the floor where they'd put Sofia—and spotted the guard outside the door.

A damn good thing, because if the man had been inside with Sofia, he'd be dead right now.

"Freeze," Luke ordered, and the guard went still. "Put down your weapon. Then push it over here."

The guard crouched, slid the gun across the landing, and Luke kicked it aside. He'd pick it up later, after he'd locked up the guard. "Open the door and get in."

The guard unbolted the door, his eyes glued to Luke's, then stepped into the room. "Luke!" Sofia cried from the darkness.

Luke's heart jerked at the sound of her voice, but he kept his eyes trained on the guard. "Get over by the wall," he told him. "And keep your hands up."

The guard backed across the empty room while Sofia rushed to his side. He spared her a glance, and his heart slammed to a halt. Her eye was swollen shut, her cheek puffy and streaked with blood. But he steeled his jaw, shoved down the urge to hold her close.

This woman had just betrayed him. *Again.* She'd sided with don Fernando, tried to bargain for her lost career. And no matter how battered or scared she looked, he couldn't forget that fact.

"Get out," he told her, and she moved. He backed through the doorway after her, his gun still pointed at the guard. Then he closed and bolted the door.

"Luke," she whispered and stepped toward him. "You're all right. I was so scared. I—"

"Save it."

She stopped, blinked. "What? Luke, I—"

"Turn around, or I'll leave you tied up."

"But, Luke, I—"

"I heard you out there," he told her, and fury vibrated in his voice. "I heard what you said to don Fernando. So don't try to pretend you're on my side. Now turn the hell around, or you can stay tied up."

"But I was only trying to buy time," she pleaded. "You don't really believe I'd side with him." The confusion in her eyes turned to hurt, and she looked so stunned, so wounded that doubts began to seep in. Had she only been trying to help him? Had she risked her life to save his?

Or was she just hedging her bets in case he beat don Fernando?

"Turn around," he gritted out, determined to deal with her treachery later.

Her eyes stayed on his for several long seconds, and then she whirled around. He kept a fierce hold on his emotions, refusing to think about her beaten face, those pleading eyes, while he used his good hand to loosen her cords. Because despite everything, even her blatant lies, he was still swamped by the need to touch her, to pull her into his arms and hold her tight.

He cursed. What was wrong with him? How could she get to him like this? He'd heard her talking to don Fernando. He'd heard her bargain for her job. Why did he still want to believe her? How much proof did he need?

He struggled to shut down his thoughts about Sofia, finished loosening her cords. Then he retrieved the guard's gun and bounded up the steps.

"Luke," she begged from below him, but he didn't stop. He would think about Sofia later. He had a necklace to find, a score to settle with don Fernando first.

And maybe by that time, he'd have regained his missing sense.

* * *

Sofia quailed at the fury in Luke's eyes, the anger in his powerful strides. So he thought she'd betrayed him again. And now he'd shut her out, blocked her off, just as he had five years back.

She had to talk to him, make him listen. Because if he refused to let her explain...

She tugged her hands from the loosened bonds, scurried after him up the steps, reached the third floor landing just after he did. He kicked the door open, and she bolted after him inside.

And stopped. The room was empty. Light from the full moon slanted through the window grates and glimmered off the chiseled stone walls. The sound of men running and shouting drifted up from the courtyard below

"Luke," she tried again, praying he'd stop and listen to her this time.

But he just prowled to the wooden stairs at the end of the room and peered up. "What's on the roof?"

"I don't know. I've never been up here." The one time she'd visited the castle, don Fernando had locked the keep. She glanced around and rubbed her arms, hit by a sense of unease. Even empty, there was something sinister about it, as if human suffering oozed from the walls.

A loose shutter banged, and her foreboding grew. "Luke... I think we should go. I don't like this place."

He ignored her, started up the steps, his weapon drawn. She glanced back at the door, wanting to bolt, to get away from this castle fast, but she couldn't abandon Luke—even if he didn't believe her now.

Her heart quickening, she hurried across the room and followed him up the steps, then cautiously stepped onto the roof. The wind gusted, and she pushed her hair aside to see.

The roof was flat, paved with uneven stones, walled in by

a crumbling battlement along the sides. Luke still stood near the stairs, his weapon trained on the only structure on the roof—a high table made of darkly splotched stones.

She peered at the stones, and her breath caught. Blood? Were those dark spots bloodstains? And was that table really an altar—for sacrificial rites?

Terror ripped through her heart.

Then don Fernando stepped out from behind the altar. In one hand he held the velvet pouch with the necklace; in his other hand, a gun.

The gun was pointed at her.

She froze.

"Drop the weapon," he told Luke. "Or she's dead."

"Don't do it," she urged Luke. Don Fernando would kill him the minute he dropped the gun.

She glanced at Luke, saw his dark jaw tighten in the moonlight, and panic clutched at her lungs. "Don't listen to him," she begged again. "Please, Luke. Don't."

For an eternity, no one moved. Shouts came from the courtyard below. Gunshots tatted from the castle's wall. In the distance, a helicopter whomped, growing closer, closer.

And then Luke tossed down the gun.

Don Fernando swiveled his weapon to him. Sofia's heart jerked to a stop.

Luke was going to die.

But then Luke charged, caught don Fernando off guard. Don Fernando fired, but the shot went wild. The two men collided and rolled.

Don Fernando scrambled loose, pushed himself up, and an awful fear jolted her nerves. But Luke kicked at his wrist with his foot, and the pistol skidded away.

Her adrenaline surging, she raced over and picked it up. She whirled back, trained the gun on the fighting men, but they were moving too fast. The helicopter roared above her, coming nearer. The downdraft whipped up her hair.

Don Fernando hurtled into Luke then, clipping his injured shoulder, and Luke careened back against the wall. A stone broke loose. Luke flailed to catch his balance. Her mind shrieked with panic and fear.

He caught hold of the wall, pushed himself up with his un-injured arm, and she hauled in a quavering breath. But suddenly, the helicopter thundered close, spraying bullets over the roof, and she leaped behind the altar to hide.

Who was that, she wondered frantically as the din grew louder, closer. The police? The Black Crescent king?

The shooting abruptly stopped, and she peeked out. A man wearing a terrorist's black hood stood in the helicopter's open doorway, lowering a rope to the roof.

Don Fernando ran toward it, but Luke gave chase. He dove at don Fernando, knocked him flat. The men rolled, then regained their feet as the helicopter swayed and veered off.

Knowing this was her chance, Sofia rose, darted in closer, hoping to get a clear shot. But then Paco burst onto the roof. His face was bloody, his eyes furious.

And he had his weapon trained on Luke's back.

No. She couldn't let him shoot Luke! Her desperation surging, afraid to fire at Paco in case she missed, she flung herself sideways, crashed into Luke. A gun went off, and a man cried out.

Luke. Oh, God, no. "Luke!" She couldn't have failed him again.

She heaved herself to her knees, snapped her gaze to where he lay. But he rolled to his side, staggered to his feet, and she blinked. Then who…?

She whipped her gaze to don Fernando. He lay on the roof,

still holding the necklace, and she gasped. Paco had missed Luke, shot don Fernando instead. She crawled to him, aghast.

"Don Fernando," she cried.

"Sofia." He clutched his chest, wheezed, then panted hard. The color leached from his face. "I tried....help you... tried..." His throat rattled. And he went slack.

She covered her mouth, muffled a cry, buffeted by horror, pity, rage. This man had used her, tried to destroy the man she loved. And now he was dead.

A soft scrape sounded behind her. *Paco.* She'd forgotten Paco. Her heart swooped. The hair bristled on the back of her neck.

She inched up her head, slowly swiveled around. The two men stood facing each other now, their eyes locked in a deadly duel. But only Paco had a gun.

Luke didn't have a chance.

Paco raised his weapon, narrowed one eye. Sofia lifted her own gun, but Luke was in her way. Time ground to a halt.

But suddenly, a cop raced through the door to the roof. He fired, and Paco slumped to the floor.

She sagged back, lowered her gun. And more men swarmed through the door—cops, civilians. They crowded onto the roof, shouted into radios, surrounded her, enveloped Luke.

Trembling now, she struggled to her feet. She needed to see Luke, touch him, prove to herself he was safe. "Are you all right?" a man asked her and helped her up.

"I'm fine." She shook off his hand, stepped forward, trying to find Luke in the sudden crowd. She spotted him in a circle of men.

"Luke," she called, and her voice hitched.

He looked up, and his gaze met hers. And the bitterness in his eyes stopped her cold.

Her stomach plummeted as the realization crashed through her. He didn't trust her. After all they'd been through, he really thought she'd betrayed him again.

He jerked his gaze away.

She hugged her arms, struggled to breathe, but a wild ache clawed at her throat. He still didn't trust her. He would never trust her.

And without trust, there could never be love.

Desolation spiraled into dread, bleeding her of warmth, of hope. She ached to rush to him, beg him to listen and give her a chance.

But she didn't move. She couldn't hide behind wishful thinking anymore, couldn't ignore the truth. He'd told her he couldn't love her, but she'd refused to believe him.

Now her heart would pay the price.

Chapter 17

"Señor Moreno? Sir? I need to ask you some questions before you go."

"Sure." Luke tore his gaze from Sofia, the urge to hold her so strong that his hands shook. She looked so wounded standing on the roof, so fragile and alone.

So deceitful, he reminded himself angrily. This woman had no conscience. She traded loyalties faster than a *palmero* clapped a flamenco *compás*.

And she was none of his business now. He'd fulfilled his obligation to her, done what he'd promised to do. She was safe, and the men who'd hunted her—Paco, don Fernando—were dead.

He turned away from her then, followed the cop down the stairs into the keep. But the hurt in her eyes still nagged at him. And the words she'd said to don Fernando—that he'd forced her to take him to that safe—kept echoing in his mind.

Because she was right. No matter how angry he was over her betrayal, what she'd said was true. He *had* dragged her into this mess. He'd bullied her every step of the way, even forced her to face the truth.

He'd told himself it was for her own good. But instead, he'd crushed her career, brutally shattered her illusions— about don Fernando, herself.

He followed the cop across the now-crowded room and grimaced in self-disgust. He'd hurt her, all right. Badly. And the worst of it was he'd done it all in an attempt to restore his honor.

He shook his head, let out a bitter laugh. There was no honor in causing an innocent woman pain. And hurting Sofia didn't make him much of a man, even if she had changed sides.

They reached a quiet space on the landing and stopped. The cop pulled out a notepad and pen. "I just have a few questions now. We'll get a formal statement later at the *comisaría*."

"Fine." He thought hard, rubbed the back of his neck. No matter what Sofia had done, there was no point in hurting her more. He wouldn't lie to the police, but he could soften the impact a bit, omit certain details, such as the extent of don Fernando's involvement in this mess.

Maybe then she could salvage her career, stay in that world she wanted so much.

And he could get on with his life.

"Five minutes, *Señorita* Mikhelson."

Sofia nodded to her lawyer standing next to her by the sunroom door and flicked her gaze through the crowd. Reporters and photographers crowded the cordoned-off area in don Fernando's courtyard, snapping photos, vying for a closer position, waiting for the press conference to begin.

But the one person she longed to see—the man she hungered and yearned for—wasn't there.

Disappointment rushed through her again, that endless, bone-deep longing that had become a constant ache, and she forced her gaze from the crowd. Of course he wouldn't be here. She'd known he wouldn't come. He'd made his feelings clear four days ago in Galicia.

And she had to stop this ridiculous hoping, waiting… Her gaze crept to the crowd again, and she yanked it back. She was coping without him, she reminded herself. She was getting through the days just fine, managing to forget about him for minutes at a time, even if his face was all over the news. Even if every time the phone rang, her heart made a painful lurch.

Even if the most vital part of her life was gone.

And in a few minutes she would lose even more.

She curled her hand around her speech, brushed an imaginary speck off her silk sheath, steeled herself for the explosive reaction her bombshell would cause.

This speech would create a furor, all right. But she owed Luke this. Maybe he didn't love her anymore, maybe he refused to talk to her again, but he'd continued to play the selfless hero in the past four days. He'd made his statements to the police, the press, but left out critical details—details about don Fernando's true involvement in this mess. By withholding that information, he'd shifted the blame to Paco and salvaged her reputation, at least to some extent. But the omission had done nothing to right the past damage done to him.

So now she would rectify that.

She pulled in her breath to steady her nerves, pressed her sweating palms to her thighs. The fallout would hurt. Once her speech ended, she would suffer the same fate Luke once had. She'd be a pariah in the antiquities world, the protégée of a murderous thief. She'd be truly alone.

But Luke had clawed his way back from scandal, and so could she. It would take time, but she was a survivor. This ordeal had taught her that.

"Are you ready?" her lawyer asked.

"Yes." She lifted her chin. She was ready, all right—ready to finally bring justice to the man she loved.

If victory was sweet, why did he feel so damned miserable?

Luke stood in his Aunt Carmen's hospital room in Madrid, the television blaring from one corner, Gypsies cramming every other inch of the stuffy room—cousins, aunts, uncles, neighbors, even people he'd never met.

"Rosa's here," someone shouted, and another old woman pushed through the crowd. For four days people had streamed into the hospital room, bringing his aunt food, making sure she wasn't alone, insulating her from the bad karma permeating the *payo* world.

But despite the crowd, he'd never felt more lonely in his life. He missed Sofia.

He stepped aside to make room for the wrinkled newcomer, rubbed the dull ache pulsing between his brows. He couldn't deny it anymore. He missed her. Once the fury of the first few days had faded, he'd been left feeling empty, with a terrible, wrenching void in his heart.

He craved her touch, her kiss. He wanted to hold her, make love to her again, surround himself with her healing warmth.

He was crazy, he decided. How could he miss the woman who'd turned her back on him, who'd bargained with a killer for her job? Where was his dignity, his pride?

"Lucas," his aunt called over the noise. "You look terrible. Aren't you sleeping?"

"It's the shoulder." It wasn't a total lie. The torn rotator cuff bothered him, but that wasn't what kept him awake.

It was the guilt. Because, to be honest, he didn't just miss Sofia, he felt guilty. Guilty over the mess he'd dragged her through. Guilty for causing the pain and disillusionment in her innocent eyes. Guilty for leaving her to face this fallout alone.

"*Escuchen,*" a cousin shouted. *Listen.* "There's a press conference starting."

Someone cranked up the volume on the television set, and a hush fell over the room. The camera panned don Fernando's palace in Ávila, zoomed in on the crowded courtyard. And Luke couldn't stop the memories from flashing back—Sofia leaping from the wall, fleeing through the winding streets, jumping from that balcony onto the truck. Slamming the car's hood on the guard, crawling down that cliff, climbing that treacherous roof in Madrid.

Damn, she'd been brave. Even scared, even injured, she'd had more courage than he would have believed.

Then she walked to a podium set up by the sunroom door, and he had to struggle to breathe. Her hair was blond again, still short, but wispier now. She wore a tight, classy-looking dress that showed off her long legs and curves. Gold bracelets snaked up her bare arms.

And even with the bruise marring her cheek, she looked so beautiful, so elegant, so much like everything he'd ever wanted that a huge ache stabbed at his throat.

"There's that *maldita paya,*" his aunt said. "The woman who caused this mess."

"It wasn't her fault," he said, admitting it for the first time out loud. "Don Fernando set her up."

His aunt pushed herself up against the pillows, ignoring the IV attached to her arm. "You aren't defending her, Lucas? After all she's done?"

"She didn't do anything," he argued.

"Except save you," his cousin Manolo said from across the room.

Luke's eyes met his, and his heart made a funny flip. "What do you mean?"

"I thought you knew. She phoned me that night, told me to call the police and contact the news. She figured if enough witnesses showed up, you'd be safe."

"She called you?" Shock rippled through him, followed by a sudden spurt of dread. Was that true? Was it possible that she hadn't betrayed him? That she hadn't really switched sides? He studied his cousin, saw the truth in his eyes and groaned.

Oh, hell, what had he done?

He pinched the bridge of his nose, closed his eyes. And more images flashed through his mind, of Sofia facing down those men in the courtyard, pushing him out of Paco's line of fire on the roof.

He heaved out his breath in disgust. He wanted to deny his stupidity, deny that he could have acted so dumb, that he'd been so trapped in the past he'd ignored the truth. But he couldn't do it. She'd saved him, all right. And he'd repaid her by shutting her out.

"She hurt you," his aunt grumbled. "She brought bad luck."

He shook his head, opened his eyes. "No. Manolo's right. She saved my butt. None of this was her fault."

He shifted his gaze to the television, watched Sofia face the reporters. She tucked her hair behind her ear, and the small, nervous gesture tugged on his heart.

"I called this press conference today..." she paused and

cleared her throat "…to explain a few things. I have a statement to read, and then I'll answer any questions you have."

His eyes narrowed on her, and his body went still. And suddenly, he sensed what she was going to say.

Don't do it, he silently urged her. For God's sake, don't do this now.

"First off, I want to make it perfectly clear that Luke Moreno had nothing to do with this theft," she said. "Not this one, and not the one he was blamed for five years back." She looked straight at the camera. "My patron, Don Fernando Heredia, framed him. Don Fernando was a prominent member of the Black Crescent society, and he used Luke, he set Luke up, to cover his crimes."

Cameras whirred. Luke tipped his head back and closed his eyes. Why was she doing this? It would ruin her. They wouldn't believe don Fernando had acted alone. And her reputation, everything she'd worked for, everything she cared about, would be destroyed.

She was doing it for him.

His chest tightened as that truth sank in. And he realized what his heart had known all along. He'd been a fool. Loyalty and love did exist. She was proving it to him now.

Because even now, even after he'd turned his back on her, she was fighting for him, restoring his reputation at her own expense.

And sacrificing the acceptance she craved.

"She's got courage," Manolo said.

"Yeah." His heart full, Luke opened his eyes, watched that brave woman face down the media mob. She had courage, all right.

And now he knew what he had to do. He turned toward the door, threaded his way through the crowd. "Lucas, where are you going?" his aunt called.

He paused, turned back, glanced at the outraged woman on the cot. "You're the one with the Gypsy sight. Why don't you tell me?"

"If you've got any brains, you'll marry her," his cousin said, and then everyone started talking again.

Luke opened the door, slipped into the hall. And hoped that was one Gypsy fortune he could make come true.

Chapter 18

By the time Luke arrived in Ávila late that afternoon, his nerves were wound tight, his pulse thudding louder than the rotors of the helicopters circling don Fernando's estate. The government wasn't taking chances with the necklace this time, he noticed. Soldiers lined the cobblestone streets around the palace. Armed guards patrolled the medieval wall.

But Luke didn't care about the necklace. He was too worried that Sofia wouldn't forgive him. Hell, he'd be lucky if she even talked to him after the mistakes he'd made.

He entered the palace, surprised when the guards readily let him inside, and strode down the hall to her workroom door. He hesitated to gather his courage, glanced at the guards posted nearby. And then he knocked.

"Come in," she called.

He stepped in, found her perched at her table, absorbed in

her work. Her head was bent toward the magnifier lamp, her blond hair gleaming in the halo of light.

And he stood rooted in the doorway, barely breathing, devouring her with his eyes. Taking in every detail about her—the curve of her cheeks and lips, the delicate line of her throat, the graceful tilt to her head.

And a huge wave of tenderness rushed through him, squeezing his heart, tightening his lungs. This woman had sacrificed everything for him. He'd been a fool to doubt her love.

She looked up then, and her eyes met his. And he couldn't move, couldn't look away. He just stood there trapped in her gaze.

"Luke?" she whispered, sounding stunned.

"Yeah." He clenched his hands, fighting the need to touch her, hold her. Because once he touched her, he wouldn't stop. And he had to beg for forgiveness first.

She pulled her gaze from his, and a soft blush crept up her cheeks. She lifted the necklace, making the tiny bells chime and the ancient gold flash in the light. "They, um... They asked me to check it, to make sure it wasn't damaged."

"So is it all right?" he asked, unable to tear his eyes from her face.

"Yes, it's fine." She cleared her throat. "One of the bells came loose, but I repaired it. They frighten away bad spirits."

"Good to know."

Her lips tugged into a nervous smile, and doubt flickered in her eyes—doubt that he had put there. More guilt weighted his chest.

Knowing he couldn't just stand there staring at her, he prowled around the table, moving as close to her as he dared. But then her scent surrounded him—her sweet, feminine scent—and the urge to touch her rolled through him again.

But she rose, scooted past him, placed the necklace on a velvet cloth. "It's really an amulet," she said, talking too fast now. "To protect the Roma from danger. The amber wards off evil and guards against poisons—like a counter-charm against sorcery."

So it protected the Roma, cursed the *payos*. He moved close to her again, felt her jump when their shoulders touched. He reached behind her for the necklace and picked it up. It was heavier than he'd expected, and warm. He traced the lines in the hammered gold, the ancient symbols carved around the glimmering stones. "So there's the crescent moon."

"Yes." Her eyes darkened, and he knew she was remembering the horrific murders, the blood. And he wished he could have sheltered her from that.

"I wonder how many people have died because of this necklace?" she whispered.

"In a thousand years?" He shook his head, unable to even guess. "Hell of a thing to die for." He fingered the stones, frowned at the primeval insects and air bubbles trapped inside. Strange to think that his ancestors had held this necklace in their hands.

"So what do you think?" she asked, her voice soft. "Is there magic in it?"

"There's something in it." He could feel the heat, the energy humming through the gold.

He set it down, glad to get it out of his hands. "So what happens to it now?"

"The government's keeping it for now. I guess at some point, they'll give it to the Roma princess."

He nodded. "I saw on the news that she survived." And was promptly whisked into protective custody. As the only living member of the royal Roma family, she made an obvious target for the Order of the Black Crescent Moon.

But maybe now, with the world's attention focused on the secret society, they could expose the members and discover the identity of the king.

He shifted his gaze to Sofia, and suddenly, the air in the room grew thick. "And how about you?" he asked carefully, and his stomach tensed. "What are your plans?"

"I'm not sure." She looked away, then back. "Don Fernando left me the palace."

"So he did care."

"Maybe." She grimaced, shook her head. "As much as he could, I guess. I'm going to sell it, though." She rubbed her arms, glanced around. "There are too many memories here. I'll make a fresh start somewhere else."

With him, he hoped. And it was time to find that out.

His heart ramping into his throat now, he tugged a small, leather pouch from the front pocket of his jeans. "I brought something for you to see. I hoped you could check it out, tell me what you think."

An emotion he couldn't identify flashed in her eyes. Disappointment? "Sure." She reached for the pouch.

"It's a ring," he said needlessly as she upended it in her palm.

"Oh." She blinked, held it up. "It's beautiful. Green amber," she marveled, and he eased out his breath.

"And these occlusions...this insignia..." Her forehead furrowed. "This looks like...but it couldn't be..." She shot him a quizzical look, then whirled, and grabbed a bottle from her desk. With an eyedropper, she placed a drop of liquid on the stone. A second later she brushed it off.

"It's real." She gaped at him. "I mean, I'd have to run more tests, but... Luke, where did you get this?"

"You recognize it then?"

"Of course. It was rumored to belong to Hatshepsut, the Egyptian queen. I saw it the last time it went on the market. The legitimate one, anyway." Her gaze met his, and she went still. "You were with me."

"Yeah." And he'd remembered how she'd raved about it at that auction, how spectacular she'd thought it was.

She raised the ring to her nose and sniffed the stone, then cradled it against her cheek. Her eyes closed, and a smile softened her lush mouth. "It's beautiful."

And perfect for a woman every bit as brave as the fabled queen who'd supposedly worn it. His eyes narrowed on Sofia's lips, and his pulse drummed hard. She was beautiful, so damned beautiful. And he wanted to kiss her, stroke her, sink into that sultry warmth.

Not yet. He forced his hands to stay still. And a frenzy of nerves churned through his chest.

"But where did you get it?" she persisted, opening her eyes. "Didn't that collector in Madrid buy it? Miguel Guzmán? He never sells anything from his collection."

"He did this time." He inhaled, locked his gaze on hers. "When I told him it was for you."

She blinked. "For me?"

He sighed then, and the guilt, the remorse at how blind he'd been pressed in on him, at how much pain he'd caused this woman he loved. "I'm sorry, Sofia. So damned sorry."

He moved close and lifted her chin, traced her fading bruise with his thumb. Letting himself touch her, feel her. Gaze into those glorious eyes.

"I should have protected you better," he admitted. "It killed me to see you in that keep. And what you did…that night, today…" His voice roughened, broke, and he had to suck in a breath to go on. "I was a fool not to believe you. A stupid fool. Can you forgive me?"

"Luke…" Her voice hitched. Her eyes glimmered with tears.

"I love you," he said, laying his heart bare. "I always have. But I was scared back then. So damned scared that you wouldn't want me if you knew my past."

Her lips formed a tremulous smile. "I want you."

"Even now? Even after all I've done?"

"I love you, too," she whispered. "I never stopped."

He searched her eyes, desperate to believe her, terrified that he'd heard her wrong. But he saw acceptance in her eyes, trust. The love that made him feel whole.

His hands shaking, his heart bludgeoning his chest, he took the ring from her. He hefted it in his hand, felt the weight of the gold, the living stone—solid, enduring, lasting forever, like his love for her.

He slid it onto her finger, tightened his hand around hers. "The ring—"

"It's gorgeous."

"You don't mind? That it has a shady past?" His eyes held hers. "Like me?"

Her eyes brightened with tears, and she smiled—a soft, glorious smile that lit her face and warmed his soul. "I'm as notorious as you are now. The papers are saying I'm an antiquities forger."

"Not all of them. *El País* called us heroes for returning the necklace." And she had other supporters, too, even within the antiquities world, people like Miguel Guzmán. And once the furor died down, they would welcome her back.

He dragged in air, hardly able to breathe around the flurry of nerves. "Will you marry me?" he asked.

"Yes," she whispered. "I'll marry you."

He slid his hand up her soft neck, gazed into her eyes,

his throat so full he could hardly speak. "And you'll stay with me? Forever?"

"Thief's honor." She kissed him.

And proved that legends could come true.

* * * * *

Don't miss the next thrilling installment of
THE CRUSADERS *Dara Adams,*
sole survivor of the assassination of the Roma royals,
embarks on a daring journey to recover an ancient artifact.
But she doesn't bargain on Logan Burke,
her enigmatic guide through the Peruvian Andes,
awakening longings she never dared feel.
Or on discovering a shocking secret that
could change her life....

Look for
TO PROTECT A PRINCESS
On sale October 2008,
wherever Silhouette Books are sold.

THOROUGHBRED LEGACY
*The stakes are high when it comes to love,
horse racing, family secrets
and broken promises.*

*A new exciting Harlequin continuity series coming soon!
Led by* New York Times *bestselling author
Elizabeth Bevarly*
FLIRTING WITH TROUBLE

Here's a preview!

THE DOOR CLOSED behind them, throwing them into darkness and leaving them utterly alone. And the next thing Daniel knew, he heard himself saying, "Marnie, I'm sorry about the way things turned out in Del Mar."

She said nothing at first, only strode across the room and stared out the window beside him. Although he couldn't see her well in the darkness—he still hadn't switched on a light…but then, neither had she—he imagined her expression was a little preoccupied, a little anxious, a little confused.

Finally, very softly, she said, "Are you?"

He nodded, then, worried she wouldn't be able to see the gesture, added, "Yeah. I am. I should have said goodbye to you."

"Yes, you should have."

Actually, he thought, there were a lot of things he should have done in Del Mar. He'd had *a lot* riding on the Pacific

Classic, and even more on his entry, Little Joe, but after meeting Marnie, the Pacific Classic had been the last thing on Daniel's mind. His loss at Del Mar had pretty much ended his career before it had even begun, and he'd had to start all over again, rebuilding from nothing.

He simply had not then and did not now have room in his life for a woman as potent as Marnie Roberts. He was a horseman first and foremost. From the time he was a school-boy, he'd known what he wanted to do with his life—be the best possible trainer he could be.

He had to make sure Marnie understood—and he under-stood, too—why things had ended the way they had eight years ago. He just wished he could find the words to do that. Hell, he wished he could find the *thoughts* to do that.

"You made me forget things, Marnie, things that I really needed to remember. And that scared the hell out of me. Little Joe should have won the Classic. He was by far the best horse entered in that race. But I didn't give him the attention he needed and deserved that week, because all I could think about was you. Hell, when I woke up that morning all I wanted to do was lie there and look at you, and then wake you up and make love to you again. If I hadn't left when I did—the way I did—I might still be lying there in that bed with you, thinking about nothing else."

"And would that be so terrible?" she asked.

"Of course not," he told her. "But that wasn't why I was in Del Mar," he repeated. "I was in Del Mar to win a race. That was my job. And my work was the most important thing to me."

She said nothing for a moment, only studied his face in the darkness as if looking for the answer to a very important question. Finally she asked, "And what's the most important thing to you now, Daniel?"

Wasn't the answer to that obvious? "My work," he answered automatically.

She nodded slowly. "Of course," she said softly. "That is, after all, what you do best."

Her comment, too, puzzled him. She made it sound as if being good at what he did was a bad thing.

She bit her lip thoughtfully, her eyes fixed on his, glimmering in the scant moonlight that was filtering through the window. And damned if Daniel didn't find himself wanting to pull her into his arms and kiss her. But as much as it might have felt as if no time had passed since Del Mar, there were eight years between now and then. And eight years was a long time in the best of circumstances. For Daniel and Marnie, it was virtually a lifetime.

So Daniel turned and started for the door, then halted. He couldn't just walk away and leave things as they were, unsettled. He'd done that eight years ago and regretted it.

"It *was* good to see you again, Marnie," he said softly. And since he was being honest, he added, "I hope we see each other again."

She didn't say anything in response, only stood silhouetted against the window with her arms wrapped around her in a way that made him wonder whether she was doing it because she was cold, or if she just needed something—someone—to hold on to. In either case, Daniel understood. There was an emptiness clinging to him that he suspected would be there for a long time.

* * * * *

THOROUGHBRED LEGACY
coming soon wherever books are sold!

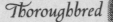

Thoroughbred *Legacy*

Launching in June 2008

A dramatic new 12-book continuity that embodies the American Dream.

Meet the Prestons, owners of Quest Stables, a successful horse-racing and breeding empire. But the lives, loves and reputations of this hardworking family are put at risk when a breeding scandal unfolds.

Flirting with Trouble

by *New York Times* bestselling author

ELIZABETH BEVARLY

Eight years ago, publicist Marnie Roberts spent seven days of bliss with Australian horse trainer Daniel Whittleson. But just as quickly, he disappeared. Now Marnie is heading to Australia to finally confront the man she's never been able to forget.

The stakes are high when it comes to love, horse racing, family secrets and broken promises.

A new exciting Harlequin continuity series coming soon!

REQUEST YOUR FREE BOOKS!

2 FREE NOVELS PLUS 2 FREE GIFTS!

Silhouette® Romantic

SUSPENSE

Sparked by Danger, Fueled by Passion!

SRS08

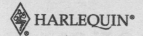

COMING NEXT MONTH

#1515 PROTECTING HIS WITNESS—Marie Ferrarella
Cavanaugh Justice

Having left medicine, Krystle Maller is shocked to find a man lying unconscious on her doorstep. She's been in hiding from the mob since witnessing a murder. She fears her discovery might get her—or him—killed, yet she treats her handsome patient. While a gunshot wound may slow him down, undercover cop Zack McIntyre is skilled at protecting the innocent. And he certainly won't let Krystle handle a dangerous threat on her own....

#1516 KILLER TEMPTATION—Nina Bruhns
Seduction Summer

Finding a dead man at the start of her dream job is Zoe Conrad's worst nightmare. But when the man proves to be very much alive—plus charming, filthy rich and sexy as all get out—Zoe knows she's in even more trouble. Giving in to Sean Guthrie's incendiary seduction could be her worst mistake yet. Because while Sean claims to know nothing about the serial killer who's stalking couples on the beach, local authorities have their eyes on Sean and Zoe...and so might a murderer.

#1517 SAFE WITH A STRANGER—Linda Conrad
The Safekeepers

On the run with nowhere to hide, Clare Chandler would stop at nothing to protect her child. Army Ranger Josh Ryan has spent his life hiding from his true identity and relates to the way Clare keeps herself guarded when he rescues her and her son from her ex's henchmen. In order to help them, however, he must face his family and the truth of who he really is...while withstanding his fiery attraction to Clare.

#1518 DANGEROUS TO THE TOUCH—Jill Sorenson

Homicide detective Marc Cruz doesn't care for second-rate con artists—especially those claiming they have psychic powers and a lead on his serial-killer case. Although Marc intends to expose Sidney Morrow for the hoax she is, her impressions—about the investigation and his attraction to her—are proving all too true.

SRSCNM0508